HABIBA

FICTION

Kraftgriots

Also in the series (FICTION)

Ernest Emenyonu: *The Adventures of Ebeleako*
Ifeoma Nwoye: *Endless Search*
Funmilayo Adegbite: *Bonds of Destiny*
Frank U. Mowah: *Eating by the Flesh*
David Adenaike: *The Mystery Child*
Olu Obafemi: *Wheels*
Babatunde Omobowale: *Seasons of Rage*
Florence Attamah: *Melodies of a Dashed Dream*
Ifeoma Nwoye: *Death by Instalments*
Uche Nwabunike: *Forever She Cried*
Clement Idegwu: *Broken Dreams* (2000)
Vincent Egbuson: *Moniseks Country* (2001)
Vincent Egbuson: *A Poet is a Man* (2001)
Benedict Ibitokun: *Sopaisan: Westing Oodua* (2002)
Vincent Egbuson: *Love is not Dead* (2002)
Tayo Olafioye: *Grandma's Sun* (2004)
Ikechukwu Kalikwu: *The Voice from the Grave* (2005)
Wale Okediran: *The Weaving Looms* (2005)
Richard Maduku: *Arigo Again!* (2006)
Vincent Egbuson: *Womandela* (2006), winner 2006 ANA/NDDC Ken Saro-Wiwa
    prose prize
Abubakar Gimba: *Trail of Sacrifice* (2006)
Abubakar Gimba: *Innocent Victims* (2006)
Richard Ovuorho: *My Grandfather* (2007)
Abubakar Gimba: *Witnesses to Tears* (2007)
Abraham Nnadi: *Not by Justification* (2008)
Majovo Amarie: *Suspended Destiny* (2008)
Abimbola Adelakun: *Under the Brown Rusted Roofs* (2008)
Richard Masagbor: *Labyrinths of a Beauty* (2008)
Kayode Animasaun: *A Gift for the Corper* (2008)
Liwhu Betiang: *Beneath the Rubble* (2009)
Vincent Egbuson: *Love My Planet* (2009), winner 2008 ANA/NDDC Ken Saro-
    Wiwa prose prize
Richard Maduku: *Kokoro Compound* (2009)
Million John: *Shadows of the River Nun* (2009)
Ted Elemeforo: *Child of Destiny* (2009)
Yahaya Dangana: *Blow of Fate* (2009)
Jonathan E. Ifeanyi: *The Campus Genius* (2009)
Kayode Animasaun: *Perambulators* (2010)
Ozioma Izuora: *Dreams Deferred* (2010), winner 2009 ANA/NDDC Ken Saro-
    Wiwa Prose Prize
Victor Akande: *A Palace for the Slave* (2010)
E.L. Agukwe: *A Tale of Trioubaz* (2011)
Chris Okonta: *Trampled Rose* (2011)
Bolade Bamidele: *Wits Battle of Awareness* (2011)
Sam Omatseye: *The Crocodile Girl* (2011)

HABIBA
FICTION

Razinat T. Mohammed

kraftgriots

Published by
Kraft Books Limited
6A Polytechnic Road, Sango, Ibadan
Box 22084, University of Ibadan Post Office
Ibadan, Oyo State, Nigeria
℡ 0803 348 2474, 0805 129 1191
E-mail: kraftbooks@yahoo.com

First published 2013

ISBN 978–978–918–125–4

= KRAFTGRIOTS =
(A literary imprint of Kraft Books Limited)

First printing, September 2013

৯|| Early Life ||৫

Habiba wandered into the shade of a large Neem tree feeling tired from the exhausting sun. She found an exposed root of the tree and settled her weary posterior, stretched her tired legs, and with her right hand, massaged her feet therapeutically as she occupied herself in deep thoughts. The other children had already gone far along the winding road and it was not possible for her to meet up with them. She wondered why responsibilities kept weighing her down as they did. She sat under the tree, staring blankly into the eaves of the wavering tracks. The sun was scourging hot. The walk to her street was a long one and being all alone, she was not in a hurry to go home. At school, much to her dislike, the class teacher of primary five, a rather skinny woman called Atika Adamu, had chosen her to keep charge of the others. Habiba did not know whether it was because of her robust physical structure that gave her an appearance of someone older than her thirteen years that really prompted Miss Adamu's decision to make her the class prefect or just merely her own fate. She, at that point, wanted to protest this appointment but something inside her throat had simply groaned a sound that sounded like 'Eeeh', which in its ambiguity could represent an acceptance or the preface to a speech, which could end up in the negative. Nonetheless, Miss Adamu spelled out the thirteen-year-old Habiba's responsibilities within minutes of her appointment. She was to see to it that the date was written out on the top right-hand side of the large blackboard every morning. The classroom must be swept daily, she was to be the last to leave the class after close of school, she was to speak on behalf of any absentee, in short, she was to acquaint herself with the problems affecting thirty-three pupils and those of Miss Adamu whenever she herself was absent from school. Of all these responsibilities, however, the one requiring her to remain in school late gave her the greatest worries. This was because of so many reasons that ranged from the fear of molestation from boys who remained behind to play football or carry out other mischievous activities to a more devastating fear that awaited her at home should she return later than expected. While she sat under the tree with a mind that was exhausted and a body that was physically sick, she gradually became conscious of her environment and suddenly jumped up like an automated doll, brushed the sand off her uniform and walked as fast as she could towards the central area of Maiduguri town where they lived. She was alone on that day because Ummi, her younger sister, was at home due to a malaria attack. From the close of school, Habiba knew that every minute counted for much in terms of her home chores. Moreover, from her guess, she must have sat under the Neem tree for close to forty minutes and that meant several hours behind schedule at home. She took the last turn that brought their house in view.

It was about 3.15 pm when she got to the door. She hesitated a while and then said a silent prayer before she touched the doorknob. As soon as the door made a clinking sound, a shrill voice shouted "at last" from within.

Habiba did not know what to say in her own defense. She was afraid. She hated the frequent rows with her mother, Kande.

Kande, a very smallish woman of about thirty-three, vaguely attractive, had married her present husband Sabiu just three years back and had borne him two children, a boy and a girl.

Her first husband Saleh, father of Habiba and Ummi had kicked her out of his house at the instance of his dearly beloved mother. Saleh's mother, Hamsatu, had for long waited for a male child to be born to her son. When Kande gave birth to her third girl-child, Mama Hamsatu could not bear the disappointment further.

"This woman will fill your house with women," she had said to Saleh with disgust. Kande had been heartbroken on that day which was her first day home from hospital, with the little baby girl. She had sat on the edge of her bed in the small bedroom she shared with her husband, her heart pummelling her little body, raw from the trauma of childbirth.

"Why should this woman hate me so?" she wept silently.

Saleh, confused at the sight of his wife's tears looked at his mother meekly, his eyes limpid and pleading with the old woman

6

to be kind to the newly delivered mother. Hamsatu simply gave a loud hiss and walked out saying inaudible things as she went. Saleh could not help following her closely behind and his dishevelled head bowed. He was a strong believer in God and knew that it was He who gave and, therefore, did not blame his wife for giving birth to yet another girl-child. However, his mother was his mother and he had to accord her the utmost respect as ordained by God.

Hamsatu herself had borne six girls, five of which died in infancy, leaving only Maimuna and an only son, Saleh. Her fears had been that her husband's name would terminate if he did not have sons in the lineage to carry on his family name. This had been her fear over the years that Saleh had been growing up. It had pushed her to get Kande to marry the young Saleh, then only seventeen.

Saleh's father did not worry about his wife's fears because he had other sons by his three other wives. It was perhaps the existence of those other sons which drove Hamsatu into her furious anxiety and frequent anger with Kande.

Kande continued to wipe her tears as she sat in the dark room. She was completely oblivious of her immediate environment. She wondered what it felt like to be loved and appreciated in its real sense. She thought of women who had borne male children and were desperate for female ones. How stupid they are! What can they possibly want with female children? What can be more wonderful in this world than to give birth to a male child and be loved and spoilt by both your husband and his mother? she wondered.

The tiny crying voice of the little girl wrapped in some old rags by the corner of the bed startled her back to the world that was her own reality. She turned and looked at it still wailing. Although she could not see the little face of her bundle of unhappiness, it moved its rag covering up and down, right to left in a riotous circle that got Kande terribly irritated and confused.

Kande suddenly realized that she herself had not stopped crying, she looked away from the child and with her two fore-fingers, quickly blocked her ears while the tears continued to stream down her cheeks. She did not want to be agonized by the wailing of the little girl-child.

She remained in that position until she thought that the wailing coming out from the rags was beginning to undermine her corked eardrum since it was now penetrating her confused brain. She whirled herself around on the bed as though she was sitting on a rolling chair, the type used by bank executives. When she looked towards the bundle, she discovered that it was on the concrete cement floor. Kande jumped up immediately, picked the bundle, and placed it against her chest. She forgot her self-indulgence and began cooing the little girl, her newborn baby. She examined it by removing the layer of covering from its bare body.

With her eyes wide open, she stared in amazement at the little creation of God. Although, very frail, pale and extremely under-weight, the child was a complete human being; her own flesh and blood, the outcome of her nine full months of strange behaviours not to talk of the four days of labour pains. She was returning the covering back on the child's bare body when she noticed a reddening around its tiny neck and wondered if it was there yesterday when the child was born. She began to hope that the fall from the bed did not give the little thing the red mark.

As she ran her middle finger over the area, the child made no response. It may be nothing to worry about she told herself and wrapped it back, only this time, she pushed the bundle right into the bed almost to the wall.

That night, the frail child kept its mother awake. The mother cooed and nursed, to no avail and very early the next day, at about 3.30 am in the morning, the wailing stopped and was never to be heard again. At first, Kande simply thought that the little one had had enough of what seemed like her favourite pastime, wailing. She continued to hold it but when sleep was beginning to overcome her, she made to keep it down on the bed, then she noticed some strangeness in the posture of the child. She looked closely and then bent her ears to the child's tiny nostrils and there was no breathing. Her heart, knocked offbeat instantly, reverberated through her entire body. She quickly tore off the rags from the child's body to enable her examine its chest. There was no sound and no movement. "She is dead!" she said slowly to herself, her hands sliding backwards. Kande did not have the faintest notion of what to do next. She just sat there looking

8

from the dead child to her two sprawling daughters sleeping on the old torn mat on the floor. She was absolutely stupefied by the sight of a dead body in the room. Her father had died when she was just two years old and could not understand a thing about dead people.

Now faced with a dead child, Kande did not know what step to take next. Was she to run to her husband who was sleeping on the verandah in front of his mother's room and incur his wrath for disrupting his precious sleep? Or in the alternative, wait till he comes in to see her in the morning? She feared his mother and her draconian disposition towards her. The old woman would not take it kindly that her own sleep was disturbed. Kande went to the door and, through a slit, saw her husband sloughing on the floor like a night guard sleeping on duty while his master enjoyed a more comfortable slumber on a six-inch strip mattress. She knew better than wake those two. Sadly, with her two hands on her breasts, she went back to the bed where the dead child laid and sat down. Her hands in between her laps, she craned her neck to see its face. She noticed that the face had a placid appearance. Pity suddenly overcame her just as two hot tears rolled down her cheeks.

"Maybe it is for the better that the child should die," she said in a whisper to herself. It was about 4.40 am. She could tell that from the light cast on the clock by a little hurricane lamp that showed the face of the old clock her mother's friend Haju had given her on her wedding day. It was one of the few cherished possessions which she owned. She looked at the time again, and did not want to imagine how her husband and his mother would receive the news of the death of her child. She had a queer feeling it would gladden them both. She walked back to the bed and sat on it, rubbed her two cold palms for a while, slipped them between her thighs again, and impulsively, began rocking herself back and forth as though she was sitting on an inclined, rocking chair. A part of her wanted the time to tick by quickly, while the other wished the night would envelop her for eternity.

Could she be responsible for the death of her child? she wondered. It was not a vague impossibility because she had felt completely heartbroken at the comments made by her mother-in-law and the irrefutable silence of her husband. The two, like raving maniacs had driven her to the periphery of madness and the result had been that of guilt and self-hate. Their unhappiness at the birth of the child had consequently left her in an indescribably bad mood without her realizing it, and she had simply kept the child down on the bed as she thought. Actually, the child was placed too close to the edge of the bed almost in a careless abandonment. She began to think her own movements on the bed could have in one way or another facilitated the fall. Kande felt sullen all over. She rubbed her weary eyes with her palms and realized the day had broken. It had stolen in on her thoughts and seeing the light shine through the sheaves, made her heart to pound. She went to the door and lifted the upper latch down but rather than walk out, she returned to the bed. Her heart was lurching so violently she could see her gown moving up and down. Suddenly, she resumed her position on the bed, beside the dead child. She was waiting, waiting for hell to be let loose on her. Her two daughters, Habiba, 6, and Ummi, 4, were up and chattering at one another.

"Inakwana, Mama," (Good morning) said Habiba in Hausa as she turned to face her mother.

"Is the baby up?" asked Ummi excitedly and jumped on the bed before Kande could open her mouth.

"Keep quiet, do you want to wake her up? Can't you see that she is sleeping?" It was Habiba, to her sister.

The children continued in that manner while Kande's tears poured out effortlessly. What was she crying for, the dead child or for her own fate? Somehow, she knew that the child was free from the fate that awaited her two daughters. She was affected by the children's innocent conversation and unaffected pleasure. How could their worlds be made easier? she wondered.

Kande wiped away the tears from her face and told Habiba to call her father. The little girl ran to the door and pushed the bolt that held it. Her little feet slapping the concrete floor, she headed towards the verandah where her father slept.

"Baba! Baba," she shouted into her father's ears.

Saleh groaned like someone hurt by something. He rubbed his eyes with the back of his left hand and gave a loud yawn at the same time, "What is it, Habiba? Can't you people in this house allow a man wake up on his own?" he said in a gruffy, sleepy voice.

"Baba, Mama said I should call you," sang the little girl in her baby voice and fell on the floor beside her father.

"She did not say what she wanted?"

"No, Baba."

"Go, I am coming."

The girl walked back towards her mother's room.

Saleh hesitated a while before standing up. He picked up his ablution kettle by the corner of the verandah and went to the big earthen pot for some water. He filled the kettle and went into the toilet, dragging his slippers on the ground, hoarsely, as he went.

Saleh was in the toilet for about fifteen minutes and when he came out he found a comfortable spot on the verandah edge and sat down to begin his ablution. Soon, he went on his prayer mat and began praying. As she listened to every movement he made, Kande wondered at Saleh and how he would not wake at five in the morning to go to the mosque outside and pray like other men, but must remain beside his mother till the sun shone before yawning like he had done some tedious and tiring work.

About an hour later, Saleh cleared his throat at the door to Kande's room in a manner that suggested his presence more than from a genuine urge to cough.

He walked into the room and saw his wife's face bathed with tears and the children by now had joined their mother in the crying without actually knowing why they were crying or had to cry at all.

"What is going on here?" he questioned, irritated by the atmosphere in the room.

"Baba, we are crying," said little Ummi with her tear-stained face lifted up to her father.

"Yes! I can see that clearly, but what for? What for? Why are you crying so early in the morning? Kande, why are you making the girls cry?"

"It is the little girl, I think she is not breathing again," said Kande without looking at her husband.

On hearing this, Saleh said nothing; he walked to the bed and bent over the edge to remove some of the covering on the dead child. He did not need to examine it further because the little thing had stiffened. He threw back the rags altogether and picked it up with his right hand. At close range, he examined it without ever touching it with the left hand. When he was satisfied, he placed it back beside its mother and walked slowly out of the room without saying a word to her. Kande covered her face with her palms and continued to cry with a renewed vigour. At that moment, she felt that Saleh really hated her. She expected that he was going to say some kind words to her but NO! Not Saleh. He walked to the verandah, found a small stool and sat on it. He looked into the distance not knowing what to do next. His mother slept in the room adjoining the verandah. He looked towards the room, shook his head, and waited for her to wake from her sleep. As he sat there, his mind went back to the child and he wondered at what might have happened during the night. He felt sorry for Kande and wondered how she was taking the loss. While these thoughts kept his mind busy, he heard movements from his mother's room. He rushed into the room and called her in a fervent voice.

"Yes! Yes! What is it again?" the old woman said doggedly with the strip of her upper lip, cutting a picture of resolved firmness. Saleh felt his mother's matriarchal response in his bones. He had made up his mind not to have any of it in this case. He, therefore, took his time not to divulge an information as important as the one at hand, he tried his best to get his mother's curiosity aroused but the matronly woman remained as calm as still waters.

"Something terrible has happened, Mother!"

"What is the terrible thing that has happened?" she asked calmly, adjusting her sitting position on the mattress on which she had just resurrected at 9.30 am.

"It is the infant, Mother."

"Eheh, what about her, did she not sleep properly? Because I heard her wailing throughout the night."

"She slept properly, Mother! In fact, she is still sleeping properly and will continue to sleep properly forever after," said Saleh with his eyes fixed on his mother's. He watched closely for her reaction and understanding.

"Ever after?" asked the old woman squinting one eye in a wicked twitching movement.

"Yes, Mother, the child is dead," he said lowering his eyes.

12

"When? I thought I heard her crying through the night?"

"I don't know, Mother, she might have died in between one of those wailings."

"You can't be serious. You mean she wailed then died and then continued to wail?" The smile on her face was like the provoked expression on the face of a wild cat. Whenever she made an effort to avoid uproar, she smiled that sort of smile.

"No, Mother. I mean, she cried and then died."

The old woman considered the matter briefly before she responded. If she understood him well, he was trying to tell her that the little imp born yesterday was dead. "Cheer up," she said, "it is for the best, that is to say, if the child is truly dead. God the giver has taken back His gift. What can we do about that? It was a frail gift anyway." She considered his face sharply, and quickly added, "And where is Kande?"

"In her room, crying."

"Over what?" she screamed.

"Mother, please!" Saleh could no longer contain his mother's attitude. He watched her open her mouth as if to say something, then suddenly changed her mind and stared at him in total surprise.

"I have to inform some people so that the child can be buried immediately," he continued without caring to look at her spongy face.

"Immediately soothes both of us. I can tell you are still your mother's true son," she finished but Saleh did not wait to hear more of her placid rambling. In a moment, he was out informing neighbours about what had befallen his family.

Within an hour, the pale little female baby was buried and only the next fourteen days saw Kande in Saleh's house before she asked for a divorce letter, which he gave in three pronouncements. Kande left with Habiba and Ummi to stay with her paternal grandmother and it was while staying with this sweet old woman fondly called Kakalolo, that she met and married Sabiu her present husband who was by all means, a more loving husband.

Although Kande's life had witnessed a beam of affection, it had not radiated to Habiba and Ummi, especially the older Habiba. Kande seemed to empty the bitterness of her earlier life on the girl as though the penitence of her father must continually be worn by her as a mask bearer, who carries the ugliness of his appearance on the outside.

Presently, Habiba looked into her mother's eyes pleadingly. As she stared at the woman, she could swear that for a moment, she saw her soften and was about to embrace her child but suddenly restrained herself and squeezed her upper lip into an ugly letter 'M'.

"Mother," please forgive me," said Habiba to Kande who merely winced.

"Forgive? There will be no forgiving you until you stop coming home late from school."

"It is not my fault," she said and reluctantly added, "I have been meaning to tell you that I will like to pay a visit to my father this weekend," she said looking at her toes.

"What? Your father? Heh! Heh!! Heh!!! People of this town, come and hear what I am hearing today. My own daughter?" she screamed, slapped her chest with her right hand, while the left, remained on the grove of her waist, looking tense because her veins were already visibly on edge.

"Ooh! Oh! Now you know that you have a father?" inquired Kande

"Mother, please I am sorry, I said so because I thought it will be best that I go visit him, that's all." She was in tears.

"Will be best? I see you are an ungrateful child. Sabiu has been nothing but an ideal father to you and Ummi. He has looked after you and your sister as though you were his very own and now that you are 'a woman', you want to run off to your monstrous father and his draconian mother. I am sorry for your life, Habiba Saleh!" she finished with a laughter that was devoid of mirth.

Habiba's eyes opened wide with astonishment. She did not know what to say to the ranting woman. She broke down and wept profusely. She did not know what sort of feelings she was supposed to have for a mother like Kande. She was clearly afraid of her and hated those frequent scenes over issues that could be overlooked. At her age, she did not fully understand the true positions of love and hate, especially when they were about one's parent.

14

Habiba had nothing to eat for the rest of the day. Early the next day, she packed her little belonging and those of Ummi and they left the house quietly. Kande heard the girls as they tiptoed out of the house but made no move to restrain them. She figured they had their own lives to live and their own destinies to define; after all, every woman was in this alone since a mother's love or hate would come to nothing in the end.

❧‖ A Change ‖❧

The future they say is not ours to tell. It is like a business venture full of risks. You take a dive to either soft-land or crash-land. Habiba had to take a chance on her life and Ummi's. She could not bear to be separated from her little sister. Though it was true that Ummi had a better life living with Kande, their mother, Habiba was not one to risk the life of her sister in the hands of a woman such as Kande. They had walked a very long distance of about twenty-seven kilometers from their Dalori Quarters, situated on the out- skirts of Maiduguri town to Pompomari a suburban settlement behind the Federal low-cost Housing Estate within the metropolis.

When the two children set off, Ummi was highly excited and did not know they were leaving Kande for good. They were chatting about little nothings as they walked along the roads meeting few people at first until they found themselves walking in the midst of hurrying people moving towards different directions. At the sight of schoolchildren hurrying off to school, Habiba thought about the fact that she and Ummi were going to be out of school for a while. She thought about her classroom, its broken windows and the potholes on its floor, her classmates and the hilarious laughter that they had shared. She was going to miss all of that because of her mother's unforgiving nature. When her thoughts went to Miss Atika Adamu she had a mind of blaming her for all her misfortunes but thought otherwise. Although she believed that the responsibilities that Miss Adamu gave to her actually caused the last straw that broke the camel's back, nonetheless, Habiba thought that fate had also played its role. Her departure or separation from her mother was looming in the air anyway. It was a necessary end that had to come someday.

She took her sister's left hand in her right hand while holding on to their little bundle with the left and looked ahead. She attempted to capture the face of their paternal grandmother in her child's mind but could not. The more she attempted the more she saw a horrid and hostile face of a woman more in the semblance of what Kande had implanted in her mind's eyes.

"However wicked she may be, we will remain with them."

"Who is wicked?" Ummi asked her.

"Our grandmother. She is said to be a very wicked woman, Ummi, but what I am saying is that we will remain with our father in spite of all wickedness because he is our father," she said looking straight ahead.

"But Kande is our mother, why can't we remain with her?"

"Kande may be our mother but Baba Sabiu, her husband, is not our father, so we go to our own father," she answered and her mind churned as thoughts of uncertainties rushed to occupy every space in her thoughts.

"He is our father, Mother said so!"

"No he is not; he is the father of Mariam and Bappa."

"Okay, if he is not our father and you say there will be wickedness in our father's house, then why are we going there?" Ummi's little heart was beating fast.

"We are going all the same because the time has come for a change in our lives. I am not sure that Kande has been telling us the truth about them. Let us see for ourselves." Habiba's adolescent maturity took the day and they walked on in silence afterwards.

They were hungry and thirsty. The sun had become hot but Habiba was determined to reach her father's house without fail. She did not know her father's house, only the fact that he lived at Pompomari and knowing his name to be Mallam Saleh Audu, *Mai Kanti*, she was sure to locate him if not by his name, she could get to him by his trade because *mai kanti* means 'the owner of a store', usually having to do with provisions.

"Our father might not even want us to come to him," said Ummi breaking the silence.

Habiba stopped abruptly on the dusty track. She looked at her dirty feet and then her eyes fell on her sister's face. She released Ummi's hand and screamed, "He will want us! Do you understand that? He must accept us because we are his children!"

The little girl could say nothing except stare at her older sister's convictions. Habiba took Ummi's hand again and they continued walking with a renewed conviction that they were doing the right thing. As they went on, Habiba's thought wandered to the possibility of Ummi's fears. What if he actually sent them back to Kande? This same thought had crossed her mind in the past. That her father might not want to see her but now, she was convinced that she could force him to accept them were he to prove difficult by any chance.

Twice on their way, they asked for water to drink and rested briefly at some points. At one of the points, a uniformed Niger guardsman walked towards them while they rested under a large Baobab tree and Habiba was vividly alarmed. She started at her weary legs pulling her reluctant sister behind because she thought that the man might be a police officer who had been ordered to return them back to Kande but when the man passed without even noticing them, Habiba's grip on Ummi slackened. After much tiring walk, the girls reached Pompomari as the evening sun was just setting and people were beginning to hurry back home.

Habiba did not waste time as she asked the very first man that came close to them, "Good evening," she said in Hausa. "Please, can you direct us to Mallam Saleh Audu Mai kanti?"

The man looked at the two without interest, pointed towards a cluster of buildings of identical paint, and told them the man they were looking for was behind the houses. When they got to the bend, they saw a large blue kiosk pasted with large posters of Cowbell Instant Milk, Top Tea with its Top Taste, Big Value advert boldly printed in yellow and white for marketing emphasis. He was indeed well known. Habiba was tempted to be proud that she was the daughter of a man known at the first asking. She was hopeful and her feet, eager for rest, hastened their arrival.

As they neared the kiosk, Habiba's heart began to beat faster. It pounded her rib cage and she suddenly felt sick. She knew that it was the wrong time to feel sick. She could not explain the fact that her steps retracted from their earlier exuberant vibrancy. The sudden reluctance of her otherwise eager feet amazed her. From the bend, they saw a group of people standing with their backs to the street. They were waiting their turns at whatever it was that they were buying. Habiba saw that the man behind the counter was dark-skinned and huge. He had a clean-shaven head. From his *dan chiki,* a sleeveless caftan, they saw enormous muscles on his arms as he handed out items in small polythene bags to some of the people whose backs were to the street.

"Wait a while, Ummi," she told her sister, "let the people buy their goods and go away before we move nearer," she added.

"Why? I am very tired, let us go to him; you said he is our father isn't it?"

"Of course he is. I just don't like us moving in on him when he is attending to many customers like that, that's all!" said Habiba losing her courage.

"You are afraid to go to him, I know it."

"God forbid!" she replied and as though to prove her self-composure she walked past her sister in a simple bold stride and headed towards the blue kiosk with her eyes fixed on the cow with the little bell strung round its neck, poor thing she thought. The cow whose photo they pasted on this kiosk must be just as unfortunate as themselves to be moving around with that bell announcing its captivity and bondage to the entire world to see just as they were coming with tiny invisible bells strung to their feet and about to herald their woes of existence to the world.

By the time they got to the kiosk, only an elderly woman in worn-out clothes that had evidently received more than a fair share of soda in its lifetime was buying a little wrap of granulated sugar. The children watched her as she made concerted efforts to avoid taking long strides for fear of ruining her wrapper and perhaps shaming herself in the open. Although this last consideration could have been spared the ragged woman since it had suddenly gone dark.

"Yes, what do you two want to buy?" a loud voice pulled the children from their needy spectacle. They turned to face the robust dark-skinned man who also had a small graying beard. His wide flowing caftan was dark brown in colour. His muscled arms showed no veins at all in spite of its daily exercise at picking, lifting, counting and handing over things to people over the counter. His face was cheeky, though darkness had made its own exaggerations; he had rings under each eye not so much from age as from having too much to eat or less sleep. The girls were startled as they stood there staring at him wide-eyed. Ummi's nose, Habiba could tell was what this man standing before them had. She did not know how to begin her story. Was she to call him father straightaway or pretend they needed to buy something, anything at all just to keep away the fear she felt inside? Even this was not easy to decide and the man's patience was running out.

"What is the matter with you two? Or have you lost the money given to you by your mother?" he asked in a sly manner as he leaned on the counter preparing himself for a hearty treat of laughter.

"No! She did not give us any money," echoed Ummi from the darkness. Habiba was sure that her own tongue had retracted back into her stomach. She felt nothing was happening in her dry throat, even when she made efforts; only grunting sounds were audible. Ummi was surprised at her big, bold sister and she shook her vigorously while shouting "Habiba! Habiba!" continuously until Habiba literally came around.

"Yes! Baba! Baaba! ... we have come to you!" she said quickly. "My name is Ummi and we are your children, we have come back to you," shouted the little girl and turned to look at her sister's gravened face.

The man's eyes dazzled excitedly with each passing second and suddenly, he called out, "Habiba! Habiba! Is that you? Ummi! Is that you?" and flung the kiosk door open and ran out to see his children.

The two girls quickly looked at one another as if to say, "He wants us". He dragged them into the kiosk, where he had more light to look at their faces. Indeed, they were his daughters.

"From where did you two spring?" he asked after a while. "Who brought you here?" he asked again without waiting for an answer. "You are welcome," he said again, "let me lock up and I will take you home so that your grandmother can see how grown up you have become," he said excitedly as he packed in all his displayed wares. The children simply watched in wonder, their fears allayed.

❦ A Family ❦

Sadia set the tray on a large blue and red coloured mat, away from the white sheepskin that was spread over a section of the mat. On the tray, there were three covered dishes of different sizes containing the meal of *tuwo* (a general name given to the main course of a hard gruel made from grains); she opened the smallest dish to wipe off the little sputter of soup that was visible on its side. When she was done, she spread a rounded knit of white flowery wool called *tumakasa* over the dishes. This wool knit was often used by housewives for covering a tray of food for reasons that range from the need to cut off the glare of people to helping to keep the food warm and dust-free. It was an old tradition amongst married women in the North.

Sadia put some final additions to the tray of food unaware of the Matron's stare from her verandah, where she often sat.

"You have kept your husband's food and I must faint first, from waiting for the food that I am sure will not be palatable," hissed the Matron in Hausa.

"Ah! Mama, I did not know you were awake. I will get your food at once," Sadia replied and dashed into the sooty kitchen. She found a tray on which she set three dishes in the replica of the first and walked to her mother-in-law's mat. The elderly woman moved her fat legs away and made room for her tray of food.

"I knew you were not going to cover my food, I knew it!" her face all screwed up into a tight knot. As she said the words, she opened the little dish containing the soup. She dipped three chubby fingers and fished out a large bone with tiny streaks of meat still in place and screamed loudly like someone stabbed from behind and at the same time, she dropped the bone into the dish with a splash which sent the watery soup sputtering all over the tray and mat. Sadia was dumbfounded and for a while did not know how to react. She was by nature a very quiet and patient woman but this mother of her husband was driving her out of her wits. She stared at the mess made by the old woman and shook her head in disbelief.

"What is the problem, Mama?" she asked the furious woman in a voice that came like a pitiful mouse.

"What! You ask me what the problem is? What do you think I am? A dog or some kind of scavenger?" she snorted with her numerous wrinkles suddenly struggling for the right of place on her wizened face.

"You do not like the meat, Mama?" asked Sadia softly, a smile forming at the corner of her mouth.

"Meat? Meat? Sadia, do you call bones meat now?"

"That was all that remained from yesterday's meat, Mama. You know that he does not buy meat every day and yesterday's extra serving finished the meat," she dared not accuse her mother-in-law directly of consuming more than her share of meat the previous day.

"He does not buy meat every day!" said the Matron in a croaking mockery of Sadia who would never call her husband by his name.

"I am sorry, Mama I will clean up this mess."

"Give me Saleh's tray I will like to see what you have put in his plate!" roared the Matron and Sadia turned around quickly and set the tray at her mother-in-law's feet.

"Here you are, Mama" she said with a sly smile that betrayed a filial response.

The old woman went straight for the soup dish and dipped her fingers into it. Finding nothing in her search, she stirred and stirred the watery soup with her forefingers. After her futile search, she pushed the tray away with a loud hiss. With the same hand, she pulled her own tray, cut a round bolus from the bigger dish, dipped it into the soup, and sent it menacingly down her wide gullet, while Sadia watched her in utter amazement. She shook her head, then with a shrug of her shoulder, returned her husband's tray to its former place. She cleaned off the spilled soup around the dish, which the old woman caused. As she watched Sadia execute her wifely task, the old woman hissed at what she thought was the futility of shrouding an ugly thing in beautiful covers. What was she covering up with her flowery *tumakasa?* She could not help thinking that Sadia was just another foolish woman as all others in the environment. It was at that moment that Saleh announced his entrance with much excitement in his voice, which the Matron did not miss.

"Mother! Mother!! At last the children have come back." There was no response. He treaded softly towards her mat. On seeing his mother's countenance, he stopped suddenly and the children remained behind him at a respectable and, at the same time, precautious distance. Saleh studied his mother's rolling eyes from the single electric bulb above her head and knew at once that all was not well. Why should he come back home with what he thought to be good news only to be cut short in this manner? he wondered.

"What is the matter again, Mother?" he asked looking from his mother to Sadia who stood at a little distance from them. She had seen the two girls and did not know what to make of the situation at that moment.

"What is the matter with you, too, Saleh? Why do you excite yourself so much as a little boy would at the sight of a little mouse in his trap?" said the old woman and hissed as she continued in her action of sending down the boluses like missiles on a dangerous mission.

Saleh just stood there not knowing what to say, he turned to Sadia and introduced his two frightened daughters to her. Sadia welcomed them but the girls could not say anything in reply because they were scared. They were, in fact, terrified of the enormous woman who had flabs on every part of her body. Habiba observed that when the old woman was talking to Saleh, her lips were an ugly voluminous heap of flesh. She had squeezed them in a tight knot that spelt mockery and mounting annoyance as she arched her eyebrows at Saleh. These actions had immediately awakened in her the reality that was in Kande's assessment of this woman. Could they really put up with this kind of life? Habiba wondered as she sat on the little mat that Sadia had helped spread out for them. The mat was on a narrow verandah at the end of the wall, adjoining the kitchen, which linked up to a small room of about 8ft by 6ft. They had kept the mat far as possible from the agitating Matron who sat on her large mat staring in their direction through the dark night. Habiba was thankful for the darkness that had enveloped them. At least, they were spared the misfortune of looking into the face of a near desecrated monster. When they had all eaten, Habiba took their dishes into the dark kitchen where she had seen Talatu, Sadia's eight-year-old daughter, take her own dish.

"Saleh!" they suddenly heard the old woman call out from her dark corner. Saleh did not answer and she called a second time. "Why did you go to your former wife without confiding in me?" she asked in a tone that was calm but heavily weighted with calculated anger.

"I did not go to Kande's place, Mother; I made you a promise never to go to her. The children came of their free will, you see, see how Habiba has grown. I could not recognize them when they walked to the shop," he said working himself steadily into his earlier mood.

"So the girls have come for good?" she inquired further.

"Yes, Mother. From the little they told me, they have come back to their father's house," he said and walked towards the girls.

"Habiba, Ummi, come and greet your grandmother. I am sure Habiba still remembers her granny?" he asked his eldest child who grabbed at Ummi's left hand quickly as if she needed support and protection from the younger girl.

Ummi felt wetness all over her left hand. She turned to look at her sister but the dark night would not allow her to make out an impression of Habiba's face. Undoubtedly, Habiba was scared of the old woman. Was the old woman such a dreaded person? Ummi wondered. She knew that she did not like any of the things that were happening to them. She wanted to blame Habiba for all their troubles but could not because she knew that her sister would not knowingly cause her any pains. Although, she was not able to explain how the brave Habiba who dragged her out of her warm bed into the cold dawn had become nothing but an over-ripened banana that was ready for consumption. What was all this sweating about? she wondered. They were only asked to come forward and say some greetings to their grandmother. Was it such an arduous task? She could not understand any of these things. So when she heard Saleh's vibrant voice urging them, "Go on, go on," Ummi found herself dragging the limp Habiba towards the old woman's mat. The old woman looked queerly towards them and when the girls curtsied in greeting, she chewed at her gum complacently and grunted like a large sow, "Saleh ... mmm, well I can see that the older is old enough. How old do you say she is?"

"She is now thirteen, Mother, if I am not mistaken," he added looking towards the girls for reassurance but thanks to the veil of darkness, the face of Habiba in particular was a pitch ghostly. She hated having the feeling that the old woman was beginning to feign some interest in her and for whatever reason the girl could not say. Somehow, she suspected it was all in bad fate.

A Suitor

Early the next week, Saleh came out of his room having said his morning prayers. He was an early riser because he had to open his shop early enough to meet the needs of the tea sellers who often needed items like sugar, *Lipton* tea or cigarettes for those who broke the day with the nicotine fume. He spoke to Sadia in a very low tone to which members of the household had now grown accustomed. No one could dare to speak up in the normal way for fear of waking the old woman from her deep slumber. This had become a part of their lives. It was difficult for Sadia at first to speak in whispers. Often, she forgot herself and spoke out but when the old woman unleashed her wrath on her once, she learnt the ways of her new home. She did not think it was right for people to always whisper as if they were conspiring against someone. Once, she told Saleh what the whispering conjured in her mind and his response was to ask her if they were not in fact conspiring. And when she asked against whom, he had merely pointed to his mother's room. This sent both husband and wife roaring with laughter. The mother had woken from the noise in disbelief and had thereafter warned Sadia against indulging her son in aimless laughter. The good-natured Sadia had promised her mother-in-law never to allow her wild fantasies get the better of her again.

That was then, when they had no children at all. She could not say she had enjoyed the company of her husband the way newly wedded couples often did. She did not enjoy to sit with him in the compound to discuss anything at all. He was always seated next to his mother and would talk to her from that distance. Sadia knew that her husband, Saleh, loved his mother to a fault. Was it really love or was it more of obedience? She had asked herself these questions repeatedly in the past years. Although sometimes, she saw him as a weakling who depended on his mother for every decision that he was expected to make, even as a man. In those early years, she had even suspected that he clarified from his mother before he came to her bed. But as the years rolled by and the children began to come, first, Baba Audu, then Ahmed, Talatu and Usman she had stopped worrying over the old woman's possessiveness and had occupied herself with just being a housewife and a mother to her children for that was what was expected of her anyway.

So, now as she stooped low to receive instructions from her husband, her mind no longer drawled to the emptiness of the rambling of the old woman. "Tell the girls to come to the shop to collect some things for the house," he whispered down to her and hurriedly walked out of the house feeling for his bunch of keys in his pocket.

That morning, as soon as the three girls Habiba, Ummi and their eight-year-old, half-sister, Talatu walked out of the house, the old woman went out as well, walking cautiously with her walking stick, she went round a bend responding to greetings from passersby as she walked along. She stopped at a carved, wooden door that was half closed. She looked around for someone that she could ask a few questions. Seeing no one, she pushed the door with her walking stick and lowered herself slowly into the low *zaure,* an adjoining room that separates the habitats of the wives inside, from the outside. She walked into the dark *zaure* until she reappeared in the compound where the three wives of Mal. Zubairu and their many children lived.

"Greetings to you all in this household," said the old woman.

"Greetings, Iya, replied two of Mal. Zubairu's most senior wives. They brought out a mat for their visitor. The women then looked at one another with long drawn faces because the last time they saw her, it was to bring Hauwau, their rival to their husband to marry. What could she be looking for this time? they wondered. They offered her some water, which she gulped down with a loud belch.

"Where is Hauwau?" she asked them after a while but before the women could reply, a tall fair-skinned woman, not more than twenty-nine years emerged from a small room from behind the old woman.

"Good morning, Big Mother," it was Hauwau greeting the old woman in Hausa, as she hurried to the side of the Matron. She sat on the edge of the mat. The other two watched Hauwau's excitement real or otherwise with mixed feelings.

"A very good morning to you, my child."

"How is everyone at home, Mother?"

"Well, very well." She did a little croaky cough and finally asked about Mal. Zubairu.

"He has gone to Bama to pay condolence to the Shehu who lost his wife," she said looking towards her senior rivals, who obviously did not know where their husband was.

"I see," said the old woman and continued after a while, "when he comes back, tell him to see me as soon as possible," she told the women swinging her forefinger to show how urgent or serious the need to see Zubairu was.

Mal. Zubairu was a man of about sixty-four from Bauchi State. He had been her late husband's business colleague. They had shared a block of shops at the Gamboru market. That was when Mal. Zubairu began business as a young man under the tutelage of Mal. Mustapha Audu Gombe, her late husband.

When she left the house, Mal. Zubairu's wives looked at one another in disbelief. Even Hauwau, the newcomer, suspected the old woman's behaviour and wondered who it was that was coming to join them in the face of the rivalry that was consuming them in the house. None of them could tell as each woman stood, lost in her own thoughts.

"Where are the children, Sadia?" said the old woman as she entered the house. Sadia who had been washing some clothes quickly rose up from the stool on which she sat. Knowing that she meant the girls, Sadia pointed to where the boys were playing on the sand.

"What will I do with the boys? I want to see Habiba right away!" she said getting angry and kicking off her worn-out slippers from her stumpy feet.

"They have gone to their father's shop."

She got to her mat and collapsed on it breathing heavily like a defeated boxer just out of the ring. She drew the bowl of water Sadia had kept for her and gulped the content down.

Sadia resumed her washing but kept stealing glances at the

tired woman who, only too soon, began to snore. When Sadia heard the first snore, she twitched the corner of her mouth in a malicious smile. This woman is a strange one, she thought. She was sure that the old woman was cooking something unpalatable in her black pot and she had an inclination it had to do with Habiba. Perhaps she wants to send them back to their mother, she thought. Why can this woman not allow Saleh to take his own decision? Her mind continued in a zigzag way, trying to unravel the mystery that could be working in the mind of her mother-in-law. She allowed her thoughts continue to run in a stream of profanity, which were very capable of pulverizing the snoring woman, only if wishes were horses of course.

The girls brought home food items like meat, rice, vegetables fresh and dried, for the afternoon and evening meals. Sadia shared the work amongst them. She was glad for the help that both Habiba and Ummi were able to render being older than her own daughter, Talatu. They got the meal ready in record time and everyone was happy.

After their afternoon meal, the old woman called Sadia and instructed that Habiba was to cook their evening meal. Sadia was surprised but said nothing. When she told Habiba what her grandmother wanted, the girl was in fact happy to exhibit her ability to cook. She was very sure of herself when it came to cooking. It was the only good thing she had learnt from her mother, Kande.

The evening sun was shifting its disc along the edge of the horizon. Fitful gusts of wind blew carrying dust particles with the evening breeze into the compound and that seemed to have alarmed the old woman who immediately expressed fears that her dinner was going to be full of sand. So, when Habiba picked up the soup pots to begin her cooking that evening, Sadia felt sorry for her and cautioned her about the dusty wind and just as she was about to explain some methods to the girl, the old woman called Sadia to take a seat where she could see her; it was a malicious intention. Habiba cleaned the meat of all ligaments and boiled them in enough stock because she was going to cook dry okra soup to go with *tuwon dawa,* a local staple obtained from guinea corn.

When she was through, the old woman ordered Sadia to do

the dishing. The children set her twin dishes beside her mat and immediately, her forefinger began to stir the soup. She fished out a small piece of meat and threw it into her large gullet and jammed her jaws one, two, and swallowed in a hurry because the soup was steaming hot. Sadia and the children did not miss that spectacle. In fact, Ummi burst into a riotous laughter, which sent Habiba and the other children laughing. Sadia could not allow herself to be caught in that liberty of freelancing her emotions. She laughed all the same in a manner that showed only her white incisors; matured laughter it was.

The children had dared the devil at last and she reacted, "Shut up! Shut up I say!!" cried the edgy old woman with slime trailing from her lower lip running down to her chest.

When the children saw this, it made them laugh even more. It was at this moment that Saleh walked into the compound. Dumbfounded, he stopped and looked at his mother first in total dismay, then at the children who were now beginning to calm down. He looked at Sadia questioningly but the woman looked away sharply.

"What is going on here?" he questioned.

"Ask those irresponsible children of yours! Children who lack home training."

"Habiba, what happened?" he asked.

"Nothing, Baba. We were only laughing at baby Usman dripping saliva," she said looking towards Ummi who could not help initiating the uproar all over again.

Saleh stood there not making anything out of the situation. While he stood there, he knew that his mother's eyes were boring holes through his back for he could feel the pinch of her stare run through his spine. She waited for him patiently to act as an obedient son that she knew he was. He just stood there, motionless, transfixed. Still she waited. Then suddenly he said in a shrill voice that was strange even to his own ears, "A child's saliva caused all this laughter?"

Again the children went agog with a kind of laughter that had a different rhythm. That was it. He was completely in confusion. He stared wide-eyed, not knowing what to say next. He felt humiliated and all he could do was walk to his mat. He sat there feeling dejected but glad that night was enveloping them.

In his helplessness, he could only wait for the children to be quiet. He could not imagine what had gone into them.

As some silence descended on the compound the voice of the old woman rang out, "Ha! Ha! Ha! Shame on you, Saleh. That is all you can do? You cannot even warn your children not to talk of punishing them against future misbehaviour of this nature?" she asked.

"But, Mother, they were playing with their brother," he said looking confused again.

"Ehenn? Anyway, it is that good-for-nothing daughter of Kande's that started it all. Don't worry, we shall solve you two as a problem sooner than you know," said the old woman with her eyes narrowing in mockery.

Everyone heard her though none could make anything of the threat. Sadia was worried for she knew the old woman did not make empty threats. There was more to it than met the eyes. On his part, Saleh was grateful for the calm that settled upon the household thereafter. As far as he was concerned, his mother could do anything she wished. He needed some kind of respite, which the threat thankfully provided. Soon, everyone seemed to have forgotten the little incidence, except perhaps the old woman whose fishy eyes kept vigilance of the main entrance. At the sound of a male voice outside, she rearranged her large wrapper and called out to Mallam Zubairu to come right in.

A stout man of dark complexion walked into the compound. He kept a goatish beard that was completely grey as was obvious from the light bulb. He wore a red and blue cap awkwardly positioned on his gleaming head, revealing two tiny ears that seemed glued to his head. In fact, it was as though he had no ears at all. He replied excitedly to the old woman's greetings and walked, dragging his heavy thighs until he brought himself to squat in respect before her.

Saleh who had finished his food came to join them. They greeted each other pleasantly before Zubairu turned towards Sadia and returned her greetings from the far end of the compound.

The compound went silent for a moment. The old woman shifted on her mat then turned to Saleh and said, "Saleh, will you not call your daughters to say hello to our visitor?" Then immediately, she told Zubairu that Kande's daughters had finally come back to their father.

Saleh called the two girls to come and greet the visitor. Zubairu was surprised to see how well the girls had grown, especially Habiba. He was impressed.

"Saleh, these children are well mannered and so well grown. Look at Habiba, she is practically a woman. Ha! We shall soon be celebrating a joyous occasion," he finished with a mischievous laugh.

The old woman was quite pleased that Zubairu's matured eyes had captured the bird in its flight. Although, she would never agree that the children were well mannered. It would make her job so much easier since he obviously had seen the point without any help. She returned Zubairu's mischievous laugh, rubbed her hands, and swayed her voluptuous body from side to side in rhythm with Zubairu's hanky dry laughter. Saleh did not find the conversation funny at all so he quickly shooed the girls back to their part of the compound, away from Zubairu's lecherous eyes and the old woman's evil stare. When the girls had walked to their mat, Saleh whispered to the two elderly people that the girl was only thirteen and should not be talked about as though she was an already grown woman.

"Thirteen? At thirteen I had given birth to Maimuna, your elder sister!" the old woman hissed.

"Thirteen is the right age, Saleh. Don't make a mistake and allow her to overstay, you will end up having no one to accept her," Zubairu whispered.

"Please! The girl is, in fact, a pupil who is only in primary five. I had no opportunity to go to school when I was young, so I will like my children to go to school until such a time when I can no longer afford it, or they are unable to pass their exams," he said as he noticed the Matron's opened mouth and Zubairu's rolling eyes meeting at a point as they looked at one another in the moonlight.

"School? Are you mad? Do you want that daughter of Kande's to bring shame to this family?" she asked anxiously, bending low to ensure that only Saleh and Zubairu consumed her thoughts.

Sadia watched from where she sat as the three adults conspired. She suspected the old woman's every move and knew that all that whispering, eye rolling, and hand flipping had something to do with Habiba. However, when the curious Habiba nudged her slightly to know what was going on, she feigned ignorance and told the girl to tell stories to her younger ones. Meanwhile, the two agreeing parties continued to conspire with every movable part of their bodies. Feeling tired, Saleh just sat there watching them. It was clear his contributions were not needed on the matter. When they were done, Zubairu announced his intention to depart and the hand that Saleh extended to him was a half withdrawn and reluctant one but because of his mother, he said good night to Zubairu who was their guest. Zubairu saw himself to the door after saying good night to Sadia and the children.

The old woman's mood had an eerie cheer about it afterwards. She squeamed and coughed roughly while Saleh simply walked away to his own mat. He did not like the way his mother was walking herself all over his family, especially his children. He knew her mind completely and knew her conspiracy with Zubairu. He would do his best for Habiba who wanted to continue with school. He felt his mother ought to understand that times had changed and, therefore, people like her must respect his own personal desires as a father, to see his daughters and sons complete their education and become something in life, not to end up as purchased homemakers or shopkeepers like him. He wanted a better life for his children. The departure of Zubairu brought an unexpected hush upon the house.

The old woman stretched herself out on the mat and soon began to snore. Saleh also stretched out his weary body on his mat but he could not find sleep immediately. At the other end of the compound, Sadia and the children remained silent. She began to wonder whether Zubairu's interest in Habiba had some kind of link to his son, Liman. She knew that Liman, Zubairu's eldest son, had been widowed. His wife had died during her third childbirth some seven months earlier. Altine was only seventeen when she died and had left behind two young children. She knew that Liman would need a wife to care for the children but Habiba, in her own opinion, was herself in dire need of mothering. She decided she would have to talk to her husband not to allow his mother ruin the life of the young girl. Having so decided, Sadia cooed the children to their various rooms to sleep. She retired into her own room and waited for the sound of Saleh's approaching slippers, which she knew was sure to come. The sound of water, provided by the kettle by her door, would make a darting sound through his porous teeth as he habitually rinsed his mouth before sliding his huge body through the small opening without giving the door any opportunity to creak. She waited for these sounds every day because those were the signals to her nightly freedom. As her mind revised these daily rituals, she heard that distinct, dragging of feet on the cement floor make its way towards her room.

The Asking

There was tangible freshness in the air that morning. The air had smelt of rains that had fallen somewhere not too far away from Maiduguri. It was about seven months since Habiba and Ummi had joined their father and his family. They had been enrolled in the school that their younger siblings attended. As all five of them squatted on a mat hurriedly drinking their breakfast of *kwo-kwo* (a corn gruel) from calabash ladles and eating *kwosai* (bean cake), the cold air blew over their wet faces sending the cold right into their bodies. It was the beginning of the hot season, when the mornings were unbelievably cold and soothing before the flush of hot air swamped them at midday. Ummi called out to Habiba in between mouthfuls. There was no sign of Habiba, she had left them behind as usual. Ummi glanced at all corners of the compound while still concentrating on her meal. Habiba had definitely left them. Talatu ran out of sight in search of her slippers. They were already late for school. Ummi and the boys were soon ready and waited a while for Talatu. After much screams from Ummi, the girl emerged from a room, looking dishevelled, in her sky blue uniform.

"Please, let us hurry up because I don't want to fetch water for anybody today," warned the older girl.

"You can see that I am ready, if you fetch water it will not be my fault." They ran out of the house as baby Usman began to cry for Ahmed's attention. They headed for school with their books under their armpits.

As they neared the school, from a little distance to the fence, they saw some prefects standing at the school gate with long dreadful canes in their hands and one of them had a notebook and pen in his hand. Ahmed suddenly stopped walking.

"Why do you stop?" asked Baba Audu while Ummi and Talatu hurried to the waiting prefects.

"They will beat us."

"I don't think so. Come on." He held Ahmed by the hand and joined the others kneeling down in the midst of many other pupils just as the prefects were getting decided on the punishment for that morning. They were to wash all the twelve toilets in the school. This was a terrible humiliation because most times, the pupils defecated on the floor of the toilets and its surroundings. It also meant that none of them was to attend class for that day. At the thought of this, Talatu saw the meaninglessness of the whole hurry. "Why did they have to come in the first place since they all knew that some kind of punishment was in the waiting?" Ummi looked at the twisted face of one of the prefects, Umaru, as he spelt out his instructions to the erring pupils. He was popularly called, Umaru *kan burodi goshin shayi* meaning, Umaru with the bread head and a forehead that looked like a teacup. This was because Umaru had a depression in the centre of his head which gave the head the appearance of a fat canoe and the forehead protruded in the form of a mug. As soon as he was done, Umaru turned away from the shocked pupils kneeling on the sand and began to walk away as the other prefects followed him closely behind. He was the Head Boy as was obvious from the red beret he wore on his depressed head. Ummi could only stare at the tip of the beret as it assumed, compulsorily, the shape of its master's head. That beret was unwillingly accepting to remain on that head like she and the others were being forced to serve the punishment. Ummi's thoughts circumvented the idea of washing the stinking toilets. She wanted to believe that they could be asked to go and never come to school late again. As they stood watching the departing prefects, the Head Girl, who had been at another end of the school compound, came to lead the pool of latecomers to the store, where they were given brooms and buckets. A boy called Saleh offered the suggestion that the boys should fetch the water while the girls did the washing.

"No!" objected one primary four girl. "We are only five in number while you boys are seven, eight … fourteen" she said as she counted the boys with a nod for each boy. After much argument, they settled for nine of the boys joining them in the washing. Talatu stayed with Ummi, all the while jumping here and there in order to avoid the splashes of dirty, smelling water from touching her uniform. They cursed their luck for that day and wondered if Habiba knew what they were facing? The fetching boys were soon soaked with water while the sweepers cautiously moved the smelling waters out of the small doors of the toilets. It was past break time when they finished. The head girl came and inspected their work. With a mischievous smile playing on her face, she picked her steps with care on the wet floors. In the end, she gave them a pass mark and almost pleaded with them to come late the next day because they were such a good team.

When they were on their own, Ummi told Talatu to go to her own class while she walked to Habiba's class to report what had happened to them. It was the last break and Habiba was chatting with some girls when she saw Ummi through the window. She immediately left her friends and walked to the front window to attend to her sister. She listened to what Ummi had to tell her with keen interest and at the end of it all, advised her sister to take her schooling more seriously.

"If you were there, they may not have punished us like that," said Ummi and Habiba reminded her that being in the same class with the prefects could not have changed anything. The bell soon rang and Ummi walked away feeling tired and smelly. There was still a lesson left before the school closed for the day. When she entered the class, her mates were surprised. They wondered why she had bothered to come to school at all if she was ill. Her seat mate did not particularly like seeing her because she had told the class teacher that Ummi was ill at home when Ummi was late in coming. She quickly told Ummi to affirm the 'sick' story should the class teacher, Mr Ebute, ask her. The teacher did not show up for the rest of the day. On such occasions, the pupils often had a field day at storytelling, clowning by boys or simply the entire class could be engaged in uncoordinated chattering. When the final bell rang, hungry children hurrying out of the gates filled the school compound. Habiba taking the lead, walked home with her younger ones.

They were silent as they walked. Baba Audu did not want to be reminded of the long distance he had to walk to fetch the water that was used to wash the toilets. Ahmed looked at his face once or twice as they walked but said nothing. They met Sadia sitting on the mat while the baby was sleeping beside her. The

Matron was nowhere in sight. Habiba and the children greeted Sadia and went into their different rooms to change. When she brought out a large tray from the sooty kitchen, the others joined her and squatted over it and soon the maize grit and *kuka* soup was consumed by the hungry children. Ummi did not feel like joining at first because her mind went back to the excreta that had preoccupied her day at school. However, when she remembered that the next meal was to be in the night, she absent-mindedly joined by sending the grits down her throat without really tasting it. She tried to focus her mind on the food but could not as the details of human excrement kept appearing in her mind. The smell that stuffed her nostrils was another matter altogether. She could not immediately think of when the horrid smells would leave her consciousness. With all of these thoughts in her mind, she left the food. Habiba looked at her in surprise because they had been taught that the older person left the tray of food for the younger ones and not the other way round. She too quickly stood away from the tray. She looked at Ummi and knew without being told that Ummi's bad appetite had to be related to the toilet washing at school. It was Talatu that had to wash the dishes while Habiba was to go to Saleh's shop to collect the supplies for their dinner. Baba Audu swept the floor and Ahmed carried the tray to the back of the kitchen, where they usually washed their utensils.

The old woman cleared her throat from the *zaure* and made her entrance into the compound. She dragged her feet on the sand and left behind a smooth trail from her worn out slippers. Sadia watched keenly as the old woman dragged herself to her mat where she collapsed and almost immediately began the usual guttural snore that was heard around the compound. Sadia's eyes then retraced the footprint of the old woman and her mind's eye compared it to that of a rattlesnake on a close chase after a prey. Where did she go? Sadia wondered. The old woman had been out of the house for nearly two hours. She had not told Sadia anything. She had simply dragged herself out and then in again. For that reason, she had not felt the need to welcome the old woman back. Sadia could swear that the old woman had been to see Zubairu. The only reason Sadia was not out of the house to retrace the old woman's steps was the purdah over her head that she must abide by. Habiba interrupted her thoughts, as she had to tell the girl what she needed for the evening meal. Habiba walked to Saleh's shop and collected the cellophane bag that was waiting at the corner of the shop and wished her father goodbye and left. As she walked, she missed a step and hit her right leg against a broken concrete, which sent her stumbling over a heap of sand and almost falling to the ground. She looked around from left to right and continued on her way as though nothing had happen. After all, no one had noticed what just happened to her. As she walked, she thought of the belief that if one hit one's right leg, one was sure to receive favour or good news; whereas, hitting the left leg could mean bad luck. She was beginning to think herself lucky that it was the right leg, which she had hit. She wished as she walked home that she would hear some good news.

The old woman was screaming at the top of her voice when Habiba got home. She wanted the children to go and wash up because in her opinion, the compound was smelling of rotten refuse. Habiba kept the bags of foodstuff and went to Sadia for further instructions. Soon the household was quiet as the evening meals were about to be eaten. Saleh was home from the shop and was relaxing with his sons having just completed the Magrib prayers. He ate with his sons, Baba Audu and Ahmed, every evening. That was the only time that he had to teach them some manly manners. He looked forward to that time when Usman would join them as men of the house. When Ummi cleared the dishes, the old woman called for his attention and he craned his neck to listen to her but, she was not going to have him listen to her from the distance for the matter that weighed in her heart was a serious one.

"Mother, I hope there is no problem? Are you ill or something?" he asked as he bent over to watch his mother, spreadeagled on the large mat.

"We are soon having some visitors. I want to tell you so that they don't take you by surprise."

"What kind of visitors, Mother?"

"Alhaji Zubairu's family, my son. They informed me that they were bringing in their *toshi* (a box or more of clothing, cosmetics, shoes and other various items to ask for the hand of a maiden) today."

"What!" exclaimed Saleh as his eyes roamed the compound to be sure Sadia and the children were not overhearing him. "Mother! What did you just say?" He wanted some kind of reassurance that she was joking. He felt his legs giving way and he collapsed by her side and pleaded with a sigh of exasperation for the truth of the matter.

"Mother, please, help me out here. I hope you are not serious about what you have just told me?" he asked prudishly and soon realized that the matter was well beyond him. He looked again at Sadia's end and knew somehow that she was watching and perhaps listening to their discussion. He looked at his mother who suddenly swapped her enormous wrapper around her thighs and looked into the dark night. Saleh held his head in his hands and felt like weeping. How could his mother do this to him? he wondered. Was it wrong for him to have always respected and obeyed her? Why did she always take the final decision on matters that had nothing to do with her directly? He remembered his marriage to Kande, and how his mother had made it fail. Hot tears rolled down his tired cheeks and he swore to himself that he was not going to allow her do that to him and his child. He quickly began thinking of strangling Zubairu and finally he must think of a way to get his mother settled elsewhere, out of his house, before she killed him. Sadia did not miss anything. Although she could not hear them, she knew from Saleh's posture that the old woman had cooked up something again which, as far as she was concerned, had to be linked to her outing earlier in the day. As Saleh wiped his tears, he walked away from his mother's side and hurried out of the compound.

Soon after he had gone out, the old woman called Sadia and told her to expect some visitors who were coming in any minute. Sadia immediately asked the children to spread the visitor's mat. Talatu ran into her mother's room and came back with a multi-coloured raffia mat. This mat was kept away for receiving visitors. It was clean and devoid of oils and water patches or other forms of dirt. Habiba had just collected the mat from Talatu when she heard the *Asalamu alaikum* (Peace be upon you) announcing the arrival of the visitors. She hurried out of the room and went towards the old woman and, there, spread the mat for the women, as both Sadia and the old woman answered *Wa alaikum salaam* (And also upon you). There were about eight women. These women were playing the role of *kususu,* a Kanuri word which refers to a group of women who represent the groom's interest in the bride's home. They kept their loads on the mat and each sat next to whatever item she brought with her. There was a medium-sized box, four or five cartons of sweets and chewing gums, a tied sack of kola nuts, a bucket of incense of varying fragrances. All items were set before the old woman. Sadia did not move an inch from where she sat. Habiba returned to her siblings on the verandah. The compound was dark and as the women sat, facing the coordinator of the event, Sadia's wonder knew no end. She picked one of the two hurricane lamps and walked towards the group. She set the lamp before the women and went back to her sitting position. She whispered to Habiba to put the younger ones to sleep because she did not want them overhearing anything that the women were going to say. Ordinarily, she was expected to serve the women with some drinking water at least. She did not see the need for that hospitality since she was not even privy to the reason surrounding their visit or the purpose of their coming with boxes in the dark night. The women began to express formal greetings with the old woman and when they turned to greet Sadia through the darkness separating them, she heard the draconian voice call to her to come and partake in the event. Sadia did not say a word to indicate she heard her mother-in-law. It was only when one of the women called on her did she stand up and cautiously make her way to the group. She found a little stool to sit on. Deliberately, she sat away from the old woman. She knew that her husband was definitely not in support of whatever was taking place that night. But how could she refuse to do as she was told? Sadia's heart was full of contempt for the women and when she turned to the old woman, her eyes were malicious.

The women began greeting the household again and the old woman replied that they had met them all doing well and that the household was very happy to receive them. Sadia said nothing as her mind wondered at what Saleh could be doing. The head of the delegation, a woman of perhaps average height, as was only obvious from the little light cast on them, cleared her throat and began explaining their mission.

"When Allah (SWT) ordains something, it has to happen. We are here today to carry out one of Allah's wishes. Marriage is a unifying factor. When a family goes to another family to ask for marriage, it is out of love that it does so. We are happy that you have received us warmly and that, I must say, is a good sign that we shall be blessed by this union. As custom demands, we have come to ask for the hand of your precious daughter for our son, the grandson of late Hakimin Shira, Sa'abo Yakubu Abdulazeez," said the woman.

The old woman thanked her and was profusely happy with the woman's style of ending her speech, that to her spelt out the importance of the groom. She convinced herself that she was doing the right thing whatever Saleh or his wife will think.

The woman who came in with the box suddenly pushed the small box over to their spokesperson who in turn, opened the box and began emptying its contents on the mat. As she did that, another woman picked the lamp up to reveal the items being displayed for all to see. The expensive things that were heaped on the mat before the excited Matron did not impress Sadia.

"Thank you so much for speaking so well. All I can say is that we put everything in the hands of Allah." Saying this, she raised her hands in prayer. The women raised their hands to partake in the prayers that meant acceptance on the part of the bride-to-be's family. Sadia felt like an inert, helpless doll. She just stared into the dark night. Her outstretched hands, almost lifeless, were ready to receive the *fathiha* that was being said by the old woman, the devil herself.

The compound was staid and sober. The children were all quiet. Perhaps even Habiba was sleeping thought Sadia and watched as the women made their way out of the house having bid goodnight to the old woman. When they were alone, the old woman looked towards the corner where Sadia sat. She knew that the old woman wanted her to speak but she said nothing. At that instant, she wished that her husband, Saleh, would come in to save her from the fangs of his mother.

The old woman looked towards her again and said, "Come closer, Sadia," in a voice that vibrated through Sadia's heart. "The early bird they say catches the worm. I don't want Saleh to make a mistake by allowing that daughter of Kande's to grow wild like Abubakar's daughter who brought shame to her family by getting pregnant out of wedlock; all in the name of going to school."

Sadia said nothing still. She was picturing how the girl, Habiba, brought the mat that the women sat on without knowing that they were there on a mission that meant an end to her childhood and school. Sadia suddenly felt her mouth open and she wondered in her head what it wanted to say to a woman such as the one before her. In spite of herself, she heard her voice echoing her mind on the incident of the night, "Mama, Abubakar's daughter is after all married to the man who got her pregnant."

"Listen to yourself. You call a useless union marriage. Okay, he married the girl but the bastard son will not inherit him and that sounds alright to you?"

"It happens to girls who don't go to school as well, Mama."

"Islam forbids it! Moreover, I will do anything within my powers to stop it from happening to my family. A child should be born the acceptable way and he should not be cheated out of what belongs to his father."

"Habiba is a good girl and that sort of thing cannot happen to her, Mama. I think you are not right to get her married off so young," replied Sadia in a tone that suggested the wish to quit being made the patsy by the old woman.

"At her age, I was already a mother," said the Matron with a loud hiss.

Sadia had no words to qualify her. Although she wanted to walk away to her own section of the house, she could not for fear of what she would think. Sadia had to protect her marriage. At that moment, she felt so sorry for the household; they were all victims of the old woman's hideous manipulations. Saleh had gone out as a protest to his mother's decision but that did not stop her from continuing with her plans. Where was he? She wondered why he could not stay back to send the women away from his house. As much as she would want answers to these questions, she blamed him for being weak. His weakness had encouraged the old woman to continue to decide for him. She had asked him severally in the past why it was that he allowed his mother to control his life, his answer had been that the Prophet Mohammad (Peace be upon Him) wishes that every child remains in the good books of his parents, especially the mother, in order to receive the blessings of Allah (SWT) and Al-Janna (paradise). It had made sense to her then but not anymore. She believed that a child could correct his parents if they were ignorant of the truth and were misleading their children. This woman had no right to take decisions for her son on matters like who to marry, divorce, what children were acceptable and what children were not. As her thoughts ran their rounds in her head, she looked towards her companion and realized that the woman had fallen into a deep slumber and as that guttural sound was beginning to fall into a rhythm, she walked away to her side of the compound. The children had all slept. She sat on the verandah, her back to the wall and eyes looking over the box and other items on the mat, glued to the main entrance to the house. She was going to wait, wait for him to come back to her. It was in the room that she would, this time, compel him to do what appeared to be the right thing to do by the child, Habiba. She believed that as much as Allah (SWT) wishes that we respect our parents, He would blame us for standing in wait and looking the other way while our parents did things wrongly. It is our responsibility to protect our own parents from eternal damnation when they use their powers or influence to oppress people in total obedience to them.

❧ Commitment ❧

The Imam's voice, from the mosque on the street, blared through the microphone as he called for the Al-fajr (Morning) prayer. The sound filtered into Sadia's subconscious mind as she remained in her sitting position, with her back still to the wall. She looked around the compound and saw the heap that was the Matron, still sprawling on the mat in front of her room. As the cold breeze blew against her face, she remembered that Saleh had been the reason for her being outside of her room. She hurriedly walked into the room, still dark, and rummaged frantically at every object in a desperate search for her husband. Finding the bed cold and empty, she ran out and sat on the verandah again as hot tears began running down her weary face. He had not slept in the house. She wondered where he could be. She wanted to fetch her ablution kettle but suddenly remembered that she could not join in the prayers because she was in that time of the month, when she felt unclean. What was she to do? she asked herself even as she began uttering some words of prayer. Was she to wake his sleeping mother or just wait for more light before going out in search of him in the neighbourhood? She wanted to talk to someone and as the thought came to her, she quickly remembered that Habiba was in the room sleeping. She stood up, went into the children's room, and tapped the girl lightly on the shoulder because she did not want to wake the others. Habiba stirred and opened her eyes and saw Sadia standing over her head. She sat up and rubbed her eyes to wakefulness.

"Good morning, Mama," she said in Hausa.

"Habiba," said Sadia in a whisper without answering the girl's greeting, for she saw nothing good about the morning. She nudged the girl out of the room. "Something must have happened to your father. He did not sleep in this house last night and no one knows where he is," she said like someone in a great hurry. The girl became alarmed as fear gripped her.

"Have you looked for him at the shop? He could be there. And Kaka (grandmother), does she know?" inquired the girl on noticing that the old woman was still having her snooze and enjoying the early morning breeze.

"No, I haven't. I will like you to run to the shop and check while I inform your grandmother."

The girl rushed to the room to pick her veil and soon walked out of the house as fast as she could. Sadia walked to where Saleh's mother laid and stood watching her for a while contemplating on what she was to tell her and how best to begin. A sudden urge to stab the woman overwhelmed her. Instead, she bent over the snoring mass and called out, "Mama, Mama," as softly as she could manage.

The snorer opened her eyes, but on noticing the furtive intruder, her eyes narrowed barely perceptibly in an ugly shrink, which sent all the wrinkles on her fat face folding over one another. "What is the problem that you can't allow me to sleep?" she yelled.

"I'm sorry to disturb you, Mama. I just wanted to tell you that Baban Audu did not come home last night," she said in a voice that betrayed the arrival of a sob.

"What do you mean? Did I not see him here last night?"

"He went out after talking with you and never returned."

"You mean he slept out?"

"Yes, Mama. He has never done this and I fear that something might have happened to him," said Sadia, weeping profusely.

"Saleh is not a child. He will come back," said the old woman with certainty and turned on the other side to back Sadia as she continued with her sleep.

Sadia stood there puzzled at the woman's bulging waist moving in rhythm with her breathing. She did not have the faintest notion why the woman could possibly be sleeping with her only son, even though a grown man, missing from the house. It suddenly appeared to her that she was in this alone except of course for the children. She went back to her verandah and continued with her watch. She clenched her hands as the desperation in her built itself into unspoken words. Tears began forming again as the sky opened up to the pressure of sunlight. She felt pains deep inside her heart, as she wondered what was to become of her and the children should her husband not return.

Saleh could easily do that if only to remain in the good books of his mother. Her mind went to the case of Habibu Musa who ran away when his wife gave birth to a set of quadruplets. She wondered what it was that goes into the heads of men that allowed them abandon their responsibilities at times when they were most needed. Why do they always forget that Allah (SWT) will never saddle one with a responsibility that one cannot contain? In her mind, she failed to see the correlation between physical and mental superiority that men so often claimed over women. She felt unhappy that she was on the fringe of being abandoned by Saleh because of that obtrusive woman. As these thoughts came to her head, she looked towards the sleeping woman again and noticed that she was prostrate in prayers. Sadia did not know when the woman woke much less when she did her ablution. For what was she praying? she wondered. Such hypocrisy affected her and she winced at the mere thought of the words she could possibly be telling God. "God is indeed very patient," she thought. The old woman sat on her prayer mat and cautiously whispered her heart over the long, stringed prayer beads in her right hand. She avoided looking towards Sadia's direction because she did not need any distractions at that particular moment.

Sadia looked at the woman from the corners of her eyes unable to discern in her mind between the devil and the creature she lived with. Is it true what the wise say about evil-doers? If you did evil things, you became the devil. Her mind rambled on. The devil is believed to be in everyone, and could the claim that it is only the level of devilishness that differentiates one individual devil from the other be true? To her mind, the old woman's vessel was consumed by the double-faced devil with eyes in the back of his head, if ever there was a creature like that. She could not accept anyone saying that the Matron had any iota of good in her. As she absent-mindedly thought out these things, Habiba walked towards her and placed her hand on Sadia's shoulder.

"Waiyo Allah!" shouted the visibly startled Sadia. "Sorry, I frightened you, Mama. Ehe, where is your father?" she asked quickly looking for answers on the girl's expressionless face.

"He is coming, Mama. He will soon be here; we were coming together when someone stopped him."

"Alhamdulillah! God has heard my prayers, Habiba," she said

and looked towards the Matron who pretended not to have heard what was being said. She continued to pull at her beads unmoved.

Sadia rushed to the kitchen to get some water for Saleh's bath while Habiba walked into the rooms to wake her younger ones up. Halfway to the bathroom, Sadia saw Saleh saunter into the compound. She stopped as though she had seen a snake sliding its way towards her. His clothes looked dishevelled like someone who had passed the night by a dusty hearth. She wanted to rush to him but checked herself. She could not show that kind of excitement that was building inside her stomach. She just stood there, looking at him from head to toe. She observed that his sorrow was heavily etched on his face. He walked towards the room, head bent low. He did not look or speak to her. When he got in, Sadia quickly turned to see if the old woman was watching them. She caught her just turning away, an evil, malevolent grin playing at the corner of her voluptuous lip.

Quickly, she too walked away, placed the bucket in the bathing space for her husband, and with a deliberate slowness of steps, found herself in the room where she found Saleh sitting on the handwoven mat spread on the floor.

"Ina kwana," she greeted him in Hausa and sat next to him on the mat.

"Lafiya, Sadia," he said in a voice that was heavily laden with fear and regret. His eyes were red, and seemed to have gone deeper into their sockets. She was eager to ask questions but thought the time was not right; so she informed him of the water in the bathing space and left the room.

While in the kitchen with the girls, she saw him walk to take his bath. She quickly prepared *kwokwo* and fried some sweet potatoes. Sweet potatoes served as the staple during the harmatan period because it was much in season. The children loved it and were always too glad to be asked to peel them. Sadia served the morning meal into everyone's dish and went back to the room. Ummi took the old woman's tray to her mat. The old woman was spending one of her endless hours in the toilet.

Sadia set the tray of food on the mat where Saleh sat and began to dish out his food. He looked at the food without interest. He was again thinking of what he was going to say to the woman before him, that his mother had really messed his family life up?

When she finished, she made herself comfortable on the mat. She was careful as she chose a spot from where she could see his face in full without necessarily being at opposites with him. She began eating with her head down to encourage him to eat some of the potatoes or, at least, drink the *kwokwo*. A little at a time, she saw him scoop the *kwokwo* into his mouth disinterestedly, which still made her glad. They ate in silence. Again, she did not want to broach the issue at stake for fear that he could refuse to eat. When she was sure that he had eaten his share of the food on the tray, she asked how he was feeling. He rubbed his hands and belched a suppressed kind of wind that came through the nostrils rather than the mouth.

"Alhamdu lillah," he whispered, thanking God for the food he had just had.

"I was worried about you the whole night," she added when he said nothing in response. At some points, he nodded solemnly and looked at the ceiling as though, seeking help and she felt sorry for him. "You must never again leave your home in that manner, Baban Audu," she said again, looking at him inquiringly.

"My mother, Sadia, she will have to kill me first before she can do what she is planning. I slept in the kiosk and had enough time to think. She wants to ruin that little girl. I will have to stand up against her for the first time in my life. It's a very difficult decision for me because of the love and respect that I have always had for her," he finished as silence engulfed the room.

Sadia waited, entombed, the words needed to sink into his own ears. Did he in reality utter the words she had just heard? She could not believe it herself and she stole a glance at his contorted face. He looked every inch as if he meant what he said and that strangely made her tense rather than relieve her of all the worries. She was glad though that he had, at last, been drawn inexorably back to have these truths break upon his senses. Sometimes people have to wake up from their slumber and take that position which is rightly theirs. Even the most loved slave desires his freedom someday. His mother thinks she is doing him a favour, her only son must not be faced with the disgrace of having to bring up an illegitimate child in his home. Young girls must be married off as soon as they experience their first sign of womanhood. Was that the old woman's only real fear? she wondered. As her mind churned the matter repeatedly, she was sure of one thing though, that his fighting back was definitely going to precipitate a lot of trouble for all of them, especially herself.

"You're right about wanting to fight for Habiba's liberty. The girl loves school and it will be wicked to deny her that right."

"I will go to speak with my mother," he said, standing up to go out. "The women," he asked referring to the women who brought the items of betrothal the previous night, "where are the things they came with?"

"I think that Mama kept them in her room because they are no longer where they were yesterday."

"I will see to it that they are returned to whoever sent them," and with those words, he went out.

Sadia quickly stood up and ran after him but suddenly stopped at the door. She must not be seen near him at a time of trouble like that. She hated the whole thing. Why could she not go out to hear for herself the big reeling event that was about to take place? She peeped from the window and saw the children in the compound. The boys were playing while the girls were seated on a mat chatting and laughing. Even Habiba did not have the slightest clue as to what had been happening in the house since the first day that Mallam Zubairu stepped his foot in the house.

"Poor thing," said Sadia to herself as she watched the girl adjusting Talatu's wrapper. They did not pay attention at their father who walked past them towards his mother's section of the house. The old woman was sprawled on the large mat having eaten her breakfast. The children had taken the tray away. Sadia was sure that Habiba could handle little things like that without waiting for her. Saleh stood towering above his mother. His head, without a cap, shone in the morning light.

"Asalama alaikum," he announced his presence and cleared his throat loudly, as though his confidence needed a little boosting.

The old woman stirred and looked into the face of the standing man, "Aha! I knew you were going nowhere, Saleh," she was ghoulish.

"Yes, I was going nowhere. I have come to tell you not to go ahead with whatever plans it is that you are making about my daughter, I will not watch you destroy her life."

"Eheee! Eheee!!" screamed the old woman in a voice that was more of a hysterical bleat than a cry of surprise.

"I mean what I said, Mother. The girl will go to school until I am unable to pay her fees. Whatever you have received from the person you have in mind must be returned, because I will not allow you do this to me."

"Too bad, Saleh, we have already committed ourselves as you know."

"We, Mother? Who are the WE here?"

"Our family, of course!"

"You are on your own, Mother. I have to tell you that, it's my duty as the father and head of this family to protect everyone. I am not accepting this."

"What do you want to do then? Disgrace me and the memory of your father?" she was beginning to play her game of darts with him.

"Keep my dead father out of this. That blackmail will not work on me in this case. Find something else to hinge yourself on," he said finding his morale beefing up.

"Are you out of your mind? Saleh, do you now talk to your mother with disrespect as if you have not been properly brought up? Whatever you say, that daughter of Kande's will not bring shame to us."

"What is it that you have against the child? I know that Zubairu has money to throw around. Mother, I will not allow you do this to me and my family."

"Family? I am not family, that is what it's all about isn't it?"

"I did not say that. I simply want you to leave my wife and children alone," he said solemnly.

"What brought your wife into this matter now? Do you want to humiliate me, Saleh? Sadia sent you here to tell me this?" screamed the old woman, her face visibly constricted.

Saleh watched as her personality changed to that of an imbecile with slimy saliva trailing the sides of her mouth in a matter of seconds and knew that she had that special ability to change when she wanted to have her way. In view of the matter at hand, he knew that he was not going to allow his mother have her way as usual. She could think of anything for all he cared. He watched as she slid from her mat to the cold floor and back again when the cold bite on the floor reached her aching bones. Like an over-grown mollusc, she wriggled all over like one in great pains.

"First it was Kande and now it's Sadia, have you ever thought, Mother, that Allah had remembered to also put a little brain in my head when He sent me into your womb?" he said, not wanting to be taken in by her performance, yet, he knew his limits with her.

"Waiyo Allah na!" she exclaimed and began crying. It was at that instance that she caught the attention of the rest of the household. Sadia came out and walked towards them while the children simply stopped whatever they were at and watched for signs of sincerity in the screams. They knew their grandmother well enough, to detect her every pretence. Talatu and Ummi were experts at watching those voluptuous lips twist in mock agony each time the old woman needed to act smart.

Saleh watched as she wriggled and cried without conviction. Even he could see that much of the body movements were for his consumption. The children had then, all moved closer to the scene. With a single eye contact, Ummi knew exactly what her sister Talatu was thinking and through the corners of her mouth, Ummi let out a wry smile. Noticing the household at her feet, the old woman changed the tune of her cry to a snort-like sound that only made the two girls bite at their lower lips to suppress the uproar that was itching to erupt. What did she want again? they wondered. The boys were least interested in the happening and were only there to complete the attendance. Baba Audu was anxious to resume his wheeling game.

The woman felt like a queen sitting on her throne. It did not matter if it was on an ordinary mat that she was sprawled. What was important was the fact that she could be stood on by an entire clan. Was it not an entire clan? After all, even baby Usman was not left out. He was strapped securely to Habiba's back.

Sadia turned quickly and shooed the children away, all of them. It was important that whatever was happening between the mother and son was not made known to them. Saleh looked towards them and was glad that Sadia had thought about it in time. The old woman stole a glance at them as they walked away and screamed again. The older ones turned to look back but Sadia was behind them and pushed them out of sight.

When she rejoined the two, the screaming woman turned to her and barked, "What are you doing, coming back here?"

Sadia stopped midway and looked at her husband for support.

"She stays with me, Mother," he said.

"I knew it. It's you who has changed my son to this irate man that he has become."

"As I was saying, Mother, the girl will continue with her education," he said without replying his mother's last statement.

After that statement, he began walking back to his section of the house and Sadia followed him closely behind. The old woman could not believe her eyes as she stole a look at the departing figures from the corners of her eyes. Since when did Saleh summon such courage as to stand in front of her and challenge her authority? she wondered, and at the same time gathered her large wrapper and tucked the surplus between her thighs. She sat up, propped to the wall and began singing a dirge and crying at the same time. The sound of her voice reached the couple in the room and they looked at each other without saying a word. Baba Audu rolled his wheel towards the woman, as he too was curious to know why the woman was singing. The older children simply watched her from a distance. Ummi and Talatu were beside themselves with muted laughter. Habiba stood in front of the kitchen watching the old woman and sympathy for her brought tears to her eyes. She had never seen the woman or anyone else sing since they came to live in the house. In her mind, she figured that whatever compelled the old woman to succumb to this emotional outburst must be cataclysmic for her words were carefully picked to depict her pains. The old woman continued intoning her sad song:

A woman is nothing without a husband wooo
An old widow is wretched like a barren woman wooo
Death is better than a disgrace at the hands of your own
child wooo
A child that suckled these very breasts on my chest wooo
Mustapha, do you see what you have left me in? wooo
I have become a mere spectacle of insults for your son? wooo

She went on like that singing of how she had brought up her son to be respectful and never to look an elder in the face and how a mere woman would change a grown man to an imbecile.

From the room, both Sadia and Saleh knew the meaning of those words. Sadia could not imagine what she had ever done right in the eyes of her mother-in-law. The children watched her blow at her wide nose and cough at the same time. When she threw the phlegm out of her mouth, half of it settled on the mat while the trail, smeared her wrapper and blouse. Talatu and Ummi looked at one another and retched in disgust. They had seen enough. That night, the old woman went on a hunger strike. She was not going to eat the food of a people who had no respect for the wisdom of the elder.

❧‖ The Storm ‖❧

The early hours of the morning were calm and bright. Within the neighbourhood, sounds of household chores went on as was evident by the sounds of voices from over the fence. Saleh's compound was involved with its own activities. The children were up and the girls knew just what they had to do. Habiba was to begin the preparation for breakfast while her sisters were to sweep the compound. From her own room, Sadia looked through the window towards the old woman's shut door. She could not remember when she had ever seen the door closed. She wondered what the woman was up to behind the closed door. Saleh was out to catch the early morning customers. Like any other day, the morning started on a cheery note. He did not want to waste any moment thinking about the problem that he had with the old woman back home. Sadia had informed him that his mother had not touched her food from the previous night. What could he do about that? He had simply let her be.

Sadia came out of her room to share the portions to the waiting children. She felt the morning breeze blow with a strange force that was surprising to her. She looked at the sky and saw a dark patch over the eastern horizon. She almost ran to the kitchen and hurriedly gave the children their food, sent the old woman's tray and picked hers and left for her room. Within minutes, the wind had built itself into a dark cover that enveloped the household. It tore through everything on its path, lifting empty cans and plastic bowls in a whirl that frightened the children. One of the shade trees lost its branch at first only for it to come down minutes later with a terrifying noise that stirred baby Usman to wakefulness. The children hid behind the window blinds and peeped through slight openings. Soon, the atmosphere changed and dusty winds from the Sahara began to cover the early morning sun. In what seemed minutes, it was pitch dark. It was so dark you could not see your own palm held before your face.

Night had not had enough of us, thought some people who mistook the darkening sky for a continuation of yet another night brought forward. The screams of people and cries of children were audible all over the street and indeed, the whole town. A disaster had befallen the people of Maiduguri. Cars were hooting their horns and multiple accidents were taking place simultaneously. Saleh rushed out of his kiosk to carry in the open bags of sugar, flour and other items which he had only minutes earlier placed outside on the bench. He closed the kiosk's shutters and stayed inside. Sadia ran out to check on the children and rushed back into the room. She could not see a thing due to the blinding dust and her brief exit turned her into a dust woman. She had sand in her nostrils, mouth, ears and of course, her eyes. She was scared and feared for the children. No one could believe what had happened to the town. The old woman remained in her room for fear that the sadistic wind that had unleashed its anger on the land would tear through her brittle bones and heart. She was not quick enough to close her windows and a great deal of the sand found its way into her room and lungs. She began to cough persistently even as her chest whizzed for breath. In the darkness that suddenly engulfed the land, the old woman could not make out the shape of even her own palms as she made a waving movement of it before her face. It was pitch dark and the sand was still forcing its way into every opening it found.

'The Lord had to be angry at the deeds of man' became the conviction of every man and woman in the land. People were running about in the dark seeking the whereabouts of their loved ones or animals that only a while ago strolled out with the early morning cool air, in search of pasture around the gutters on the street. There was confusion everywhere. In their various hiding places, Muslims and Christians alike began saying what seemed like their last prayers. The Muslims pulled at their *Chasbi* (prayer beads) asking forgiveness from Almighty Allah while Christians knelt down in deep supplication as they were sure that the moment of the prophesied Armageddon was at hand and they waited patiently for the trumpet sound that was to usher in the re-awakening and the long awaited day of judgment. It was a day of reckoning. Everyone was on his or her own; fathers would not know their children. They waited patiently for what they all thought was the final moment while the darkness thickened and the air became more frigid. They heard some distant cracking noises that were frightening and they all wondered what it could be. The old woman could not hold on the quantity of dust she had inhaled and the airlessness of the atmosphere, coupled with the lack of energy due to the fact that she had eaten nothing the previous night, all summed up to deprive her of consciousness and she collapsed on the heap of dust on the floor. As suddenly as it had started, the sand storm began to settle down and the atmosphere began to give way to rays from the sun. The nightmare took a period of twenty minutes but in reality, it seemed for eternity. When the cloud was clear enough, people waited for the brave to venture out first. They were not sure whether they were going to see the world they had been used to or in fact, were about to face an unknown planet or perhaps, it was the fall of a comet from its heavenly abode that had thrown them into the trance-like experience. One after the other, people began to move out of their hiding places into the frenzy of seeking their loved ones and counting their losses. With the slightest visibility, Saleh ran home blindly, running over confused people or jumping over fallen tree trunks and household wares that were flung over people's fences. He had never witnessed anything like that in his over forty years. When he got to the house, he made for the children's room, as he was shouting names of Sadia, Habiba, Ahmed and so forth without knowing which to look out for. Sadia also ran out on hearing his voice.

She came out from the room, beating the dust off herself with one of her wrappers. She followed Saleh closely behind as he entered the children's room. They were all still crunched under a large tarpaulin that hardly allowed air passage. Dropping the wrapper quickly, she helped him pull the synthetic covering off them and faced the nightmare that was to be remembered for a lifetime. Several of the children were limp and could not move. Sadia went hysterical and began to scream at the sight of what had happened. At the same time, they dragged the children one after the other out of the room and unto the verandah. Sadia saw Habiba's head move, and still strapped on her back was the baby, Usman. She pulled out the baby and held him to her breast; his limpness startled her. She shook his tiny body vigorously and at the same time, desperately, she prised his eyes with her thumb and forefinger, but only the white of the eyes were obvious. When realization dawned on her, she held the lifeless body of her baby close to her heart and let out a cry that had no semblance to the normal crying associated with humans. Saleh looked towards Sadia, then rushed to the water drum inside the kitchen and came out with a pail full and without much thought, poured the water over the unconscious children and again, rushed for more until he had drenched them all and water was flowing everywhere. Habiba was the first to sit up and was followed by Talatu then Baba Audu and then Ahmed moved his feet after a while. In her delirium, Habiba saw Ummi still motionless and she rushed to her side and shook her vigorously while at the same time, shouting her name. Seeing what was going on, Saleh rushed back into the kitchen and came back with another pail full of water, which he splashed on the girl. As the water slapped her face, Ummi made a movement and both father and child knew that their fears were allayed. He then quickly turned his attention to Sadia's cries and the baby she was cradling in her arms. He took the child from her and noticing the lifelessness in the child, his mind went back several years ago when Kande's newborn daughter had died. With one hand, he held on to the dead child while with the other, he touched Sadia on the shoulder tenderly but Sadia would not be consoled.

All the revived children were seated in the now muddy floor watching their father as he whispered soothing phrases from the Noble Qur'an to help her accept the moment as an act from God. They wondered why she was wailing so much. As he stood there, Saleh's mind raced to his mother and he quickly returned the dead child to its mother and rushed to see if his mother was well. It was only as he rushed to her section of the house that he realized that he had not seen or heard from her since the previous evening. He pushed the door open with a bang, the room was squalid, like it had been abandoned or not been lived in for long. He suddenly realized that he had not been in the room for very long. How could he when his mother always sat on the verandah and gave directives to everyone? The room was still dark in spite of the sun outside. He went first to the heavy window blinds and pulled them wide open as he called out hurriedly to her. When he turned around, he saw on the dusty floor, sprawled in a miserable heap, his mother, lying unconscious. He ran to her side shouting, "Mother, Mother," repeatedly but the old woman would not even move. He bent over to listen to her heartbeat and a slight movement from her chest signalled that he was not late in coming. In desperation, he ruffled his head, felt like screaming but thought otherwise and rushed out of the room to where Sadia and the children still sat. He picked the bucket in a sweep and dashed to the kitchen and soon he was standing over his drenched mother. She was still motionless. He shook her continuously and still, the old woman would not move. He bent over her and felt her heartbeat again; he could hear a tiny flicker of movement or sound from her chest still. He knew he had to do something fast. In a flash, he ran out of the house into the street, maddening with people crying, running or being rushed to the hospital. He had to get help quick for his mother. He waved at a car he thought was a taxi but the car sped past him, probably rushing to count his own losses or those of his kins. He ran across the road to the right side and everyone in sight was running towards one point or the other. He could not think just then. Several motorbikes also sped past him and he wondered how an unconscious woman could be placed on a bike and he knew that it had to be a car, but where was he to get a car when every car owner would be facing his own toll of sorrows? At one corner, he saw a car beneath a large neem trunk. The tree had fallen and the damage was enormous, Saleh had no time to waste thinking about someone else's misfortune. He stopped yet another car that slowed down to negotiate a bend but the driver simply hissed at him and sped off like all the others. The street was dense with the heavy breathing of hurrying and scurrying men and of women who could not accept the event of the moment as an act of God but must wail and tear at their hairs and clothes in public. His mind flashed back and he remembered Sadia and the dead child back home and again, ran across the road to see what was happening to her and the children and most of all, his mother. As he neared the entrance to his house, his neighbour, Mallam Hashimu, was reversing his Volkswagen Golf out of its parking space onto the street. He quickly ran to him, "Mallam Hashimu," he said with a sad yet passionate timbre in his voice that even Hashimu, in spite of his own problems, was ready to listen as Saleh made a plea for his mother to be taken to the hospital.

"As a matter of fact, I am also going to the hospital, get her into the car fast."

If Saleh heard the last word, Hashimu could not tell. In what seemed minutes, Saleh with the help of Habiba, Ummi and Baba Audu, moved the old woman, dripping muddy water, onto the back seat of Hashimu's car where Hashimu's own son sat. The boy, Adamu, had a gaping slash on his forehead that was bleeding profusely into an old wrapper his mother had placed on the cut. Saleh quickly opened the front seat and joined Hashimu while the boy's mother sat in the back seat and helped to support the old woman. Soon, the car left the street on its way to the University of Maiduguri Teaching Hospital located at another end of the town. It made its way through the many bends of the Murtala Mohammed Federal Housing Estate. As the car sped on, Saleh watched in wonder how the town had suddenly been transformed into an emergency within a twinkle of an eye.

Back home, Sadia did not know what to do with the dead child. She collapsed onto a mat and continued crying and this time, all the children joined in the sorrow. Habiba looked at the little wrapped bundle that Sadia had deposited at one end of the verandah and felt a deep sense of loss. She could not believe that she was never going to strap the little boy on her back again. She felt as though she was responsible for his death. Could she have strangled him on her back? Or was it the dust that had choked him to death? Could she have fallen on her back and squashed the boy to death? She could not extricate herself from blame as she focused her gaze on the old flowered wrapper print in which the body was wrapped. Her child's mind could not understand the intricate logic of airlessness or suffocation. What kept recurring in her mind was the simple fact that from whatever position, his body was pulled from her back where he was strapped to the end.

As they all cried, Ahmed looked at Talatu's wet face and whispered, "Why is Usman not crying with us?" and she looked at him with a reprimanding wink. Not satisfied, he again moved closer to her, nudged at her ribs a little harder and then he received a stern warning "shhhhhhh" and he reclined against the wall, embarrassed.

Sadia cried on as she thought of what had to be done since Saleh had taken his mother to the hospital. She was not sure the old woman was going to make it too and the thought made her cry more with a new vigour and the children picked up the tremor in her voice and renewed the strength of their own crying until they had subdued every other sound in the compound.

With difficulty finding a parking space, the car pulled up in front of a crowded Accident and Emergency Ward. Like the new arrivals, the numerous emergencies created by the storm had been rushed to the hospital for attention. People carrying their wounded relatives were hurrying here and there while hospital attendants and doctors had their hands full. It was a Tsunami of a kind. The ratio of doctors and nurses was a ridiculous one even before the storm; after the storm, however, the hospital workers felt choked up. There were only three doctors on ground to attend to over five hundred emergencies. The doctors had immediately asked the Chief Medical Officer to draft some more hands to the ward. As they awaited the arrivals of the doctors and nurses, they attended only to severe cases and ignored the minor ones even when they had to skip the next person on the queue. This made some of the early callers to say many disgruntled words, especially when they heard that like everywhere else, the hospital too had been hit severely by the storm. A section that was quarantined for patients with the HIV/AIDS had collapsed and killed seven patients. When some of the people heard the news, they simply laughed. One of the listeners wondered why they were laughing, the answer he got was, "Please, my friend, let's talk of human beings," that aroused more interest from the people. Another man asked why the first man talked of the dead as though they were mere rabbits, he was told to shut up. The general belief was that the victims were better off dead anyway.

Saleh was the first to dash out of the car to open the back

seat. Habibu's wife and son came out when Saleh got hold of his still unconscious mother. He could not carry her alone and all around him, everyone was in a great hurry to offer a helping hand. Hashimu first ran into the ward to know if, in fact, doctors were on ground and attending to patients. When he entered the hall, apart from the darkness that confronted him, he was hit by a strong smell of blood mixed with sweat and his stomach churned immediately. He hurried out of the place and joined the others by the car.

"It is terrible in there," he said, shaking his head sadly. Saleh did not know what he meant by the statement, all he wanted was to get a doctor to see his mother before long.

"Did you see the doctors?" Saleh asked.

"The crowd inside is thick."

"I have to get a doctor to see my mother, Mallam Hashimu. Please, could you wait for me to go speak with anyone of them?" he pleaded.

"We'll wait for you because I will take Adamu to Nakowa Specialist. The patients here are definitely too many for the doctors and nurses to effectively handle," said Hashimu with a grimace that expressed his regrets in the system that was unable to plan for its citizens in times of peace much less in troubled times like the one they were faced with. As he watched Saleh going into the dingy hall, he wondered at the commitment of the doctors who were still working to save lives in spite of their working conditions. He peeped at his wife and son still seated on the back seat. The wound on the boy's face was still bleeding but not as profusely as it did earlier.

Hashimu's wife, Hajara, was still supporting the old woman with her own weight in a sitting position.

"Is she breathing?" Hashimu asked his wife.

"Of course, she is. A bit too faintly. I hope that we can get someone to look at her because she may not withstand this rigour much longer," she said sadly, watching the old woman's contorted face.

"She is an ox."

"She is strong," she replied with a nod and saw Saleh running towards the car with two male nurses in dirty uniforms and carrying a stretcher, making their way to the car.

"May Allah bless you abundantly," he said to Hashimu as soon as he got to the car and quickly turned. With the help of Hashimu, Hajara and the two nurses, the woman was immediately laid on the stretcher and was rushed to the ward.

"I will see you later, Mallam Saleh, I will take the boy to get some treatment as well. May Allah grant her quick recovery," he said to Saleh whose back was already turned to them as he ran after the stretcher into the ward. Hajara watched sadly as the old woman was taken away and thought that, perhaps, they were never going to see her again.

The old woman was deposited onto a bed that was badly stained with blood from a patient that had to be transferred to the floor of an adjoining room because every little space in the ward was in use. It was an emergency even people of forty and above had never witnessed. A young female doctor of no more than thirty quickly walked to the old woman and placed her stethoscope on her chest through the lower cut of the old woman's flapping sleeves. She bent over the woman as she listened to the beating of her heart and pulse. She had to work alone because there were no extra hands to draft or to assist her in the examination of a patient. In fact, at some points in the ward, nurses had had to assume the position of doctors and do those things that were the sole duties of doctors. Saleh remained by the bed. He saw the blood but could say or do nothing about it, after all, they were all faced by the same fate. He wished his mother would recover her consciousness and not die just like that. He knew that he could not take another loss, not just then. As he thought about the fate that had befallen him, he remembered that he had a dead child back home awaiting his arrival for the burial arrangements to be made. He was thinking of what was going to happen in the next few hours when the voice of the doctor drifted into his own consciousness in the midst of the assortment of noises. Startled, he realized that she had been saying something to him, which he did not hear. From a little distance, he heard someone skulking and wailing. He turned quickly, not to the doctor whose voice was next to him but to the direction of the crying.

"Why is he crying?" he asked before he recollected himself in the hard stare of the woman doctor.

"Mallam!" she cried out finally. "I have no time to waste here while you stand on your feet and daydream. I was telling you that your mother has had a severe stroke. Did she fall from a height?" she asked.

"I cannot tell, Doctor. I found her lying on the floor after the storm and rushed her here."

"We are going to move her to the Intensive Care Unit (ICU). We need to conduct some scans on her as soon as possible then we will wait until she regains consciousness. I do hope that you can quickly raise the sum of fifty thousand naira before 5 pm today?" said the doctor in a matter of fact voice.

Saleh's heart missed a beat when he heard the sum he was to pay. He looked perplexed and wondered at how much time he had before 5 pm. His heartbeat pummelled through his body and he feared that she was going to see his shock and change her mind on whatever treatment she was arranging for his mother. He was not sure he could raise that kind of money from the shop but he could not disclose that to the doctor whose trust in him was obvious.

"That will be good, Doctor, thank you so much; I will be here by the time." Saleh did not want to commit himself in totality by mentioning the time.

If the doctor caught the reservation in his reply and tone, she said nothing. As she walked away to get some hands to help in the movement to the ICU, Saleh went closer to his mother and looked closely at her twisted face. She probably was discontented with her life since yesterday when he had disobeyed her for the first time ever. How could he have agreed with her when he knew that she was on the verge of destroying the life of a young promising girl that loved school? She was pale and he noticed a contortion on the left side of her face. The face seemed slanted to the left. Had she always had the stiffness or was it a new development? He could not remember when he had looked at his mother at such a close range since he was a kid. In the past years, he had often seen her only in the nights when he got back from the shop to join the family for the evening meals. In the mornings, he went out soon after the Al-Fajr prayers, which are offered between the hours of 5.00-5.15 am. He had no way of confirming the change. He observed that she had sand in every possible opening on her face, which made her look like a lost adventurer from the desert. Her lips were dry and ashen. His thought was suddenly cut short with the arrival of the doctor and a different nurse who began to wheel the bed through the frenzied crowd of patients that had swelled in the short time that his attention was on his mother. He followed both doctor and nurse as the bed carrying his mother was hurrying through long crowded corridors striped with long lines of colours with arrowheads that, if followed, would lead to different parts of the hospital. They hurried on as people shortly forgot their own problems and looked at the bed as it raced along. Someone was more critical than their own case they thought and thanked God for His mercies and said silent prayers for all the sick. The bed made yet another turn, they were in a dark tunnel-like passage that was actually sloping, and the gradient was towards the way they came and that made pushing the bed upward a little difficult for the nurse. They were going up to the first or perhaps second floor. Saleh quickly ran to help push the bed for it was about undermining the strength of the nurse. The whole thing was like walking up a hill with a load twice as heavy as you were. The old woman was a mass of flesh. They pushed on until they got to another long, narrow corridor and as they rolled by, Saleh saw a large sign that told him they had arrived at the ICU. The place was a lot cleaner than most parts of the hospital. He was asked to change from his slippers into one of the several he saw in a small space adjoining the ICU. The nurse and doctor also changed their shoes; only, theirs were made of wooden soles and white, man-made tops. In the ICU, they met two attendants who quickly transferred the old woman to another bed and immediately began connecting her to a mask placed on her face and some other gadgets to assist her breathing. She was also connected to some infusion devices on both arms. Saleh was glad for the help and he was relieved that his mother was safe. The doctor spoke to one of the attendants aside and after, told Saleh that his mother was to be taken care of by the ICU staff until she got out of danger. However, he needed to follow her to get her folder and pay part of the bills. He had thought that the 10,000 naira in his pocket could settle the entire hospital bill but the doctor had instilled the fear of the unknown in his heart. Why had he not known that the bill for a stroke patient was going to be different from that of someone suffering from malaria? He had never had a major sickness to support in his family. His father had died in his sleep without having complained of a headache before he slept. He began to appreciate the doctor. Most doctors would have asked for some deposits first before even touching the sick. He looked at his mother for a moment before following the doctor out of the ICU. As he walked a step or two behind her, he wondered what could happen in the unfortunate event of his inability to raise the fifty thousand. Was his mother to be thrown out to die in the open ward? He walked in silence as his thoughts went ahead scrutinizing the fate before him. When they got to her office, a number of people were waiting. Some cuddled their young children, others bent in two, perhaps in great pains. The storm had really dealt a great blow on the town. She studied the people at a glance, turned back to Saleh and quickly pointed her index finger, directing him to follow a green arrowed line on the floor of the long corridor to its end.

"Follow the green line; it will take you to the Documentation Department. When you get her registered, a staff will accompany you back to this office because I have to bill you on the folder," she said without a smile.

"Okay, Doctor," replied Saleh and began heading towards the green line and its many bends, to its final destination. As he walked, constantly looking down so as not to miss the track, he saw people still hurrying in search of help from the few available doctors. The hospital had never witnessed such an upheaval of events. Saleh walked as people around him were screaming here and cursing there, the smell of sweat and blood continued to fill the air. People quickly brushed him by and hurried along unknowing; everyone was hurrying to solve his own personal emergency.

⟩ After the Storm ⟨

Sadia sat on the floor not looking at the corner where she had kept the dead child. It was still in its wrapping like an unwanted gift which was never going to be opened. Her tear-stained face had a distant look. It was hours since they were struck by the storm. She wondered where Saleh was or what he could be doing. Was his mother also dead? She could not provide answers to her worries. The children had gone out of the room. Ahmed perched on the fallen tree in the compound while Baba Audu went around looking for some rope to hang a swing. The girls sat on the verandah and talked in low tones. They talked about their grandmother and Habiba told them about their dead baby brother no one was ever going to see. They were sad to know that they were going to have no baby in the house to play with anymore.

The sun was already getting hot when Habiba called on her sisters to help tidy up the compound. Talatu picked the tray of fried sweet potatoes that was meant to be their breakfast; it was a heap of fine sand. The children had not eaten a morsel since morning. She began to sweep while Ummi and Habiba picked cans, pots and the like that the storm had displaced everywhere. The boys played on without concern for what was going on. Sadia could hear the sounds made by the children but would not come out. She was not crying, just sitting there, letting out little shrieks now and again and wearing that distant look all the time. In her mind, she revisited her experiences during the pregnancy that brought forth the child that had just been whisked away from her by the cruel hands of death. How, in spite of her condition, the old woman would make demands of her that were unwarranted. How she went into labour and yet the child would not come for four days. How neighbours advised that she be taken to the hospital and how Saleh, following his mother's advice, had refused until the last minute when he knew that he was going to be blamed for her death. Again, she wondered if he was coming to bury his child or if perhaps, he expected her to go out and call in the neighbours. She needed to protect the goings-on of the household and that to her, was the right time. She had to wait for him to come back, even if it took him the whole day. This resolve kept her seated on the spot like a cobra, entombed, calculating and waiting.

The compound was regaining its appearance except for the fallen Neem tree whose greenish seeds were littered around due to the activities of Baba Audu and Ahmed. Habiba had swept Sadia's bedroom and was busy in the smaller room when they all heard the screams of "Baba, Baba, Baba ..." from the boys. All rushed out to meet him. The younger ones jumped on him while Habiba and Ummi just went close to him and their empathy infused into his pores and tears came to his eyes.

"Where is your mother?" he asked the excited children and doing his best to hide his emotions.

"Mother is in the room," it was Ahmed who shouted the answer.

"In the room," several voices replied.

He extricated himself from their hold and without being told in which of the rooms she was, walked briskly to the children's room where some hours ago, they had faced the new world that was to be their reality. At the door, he stopped and made the remaining space slowly towards the woman crouched on the floor. She had renewed her crying on hearing his voice. He walked to her calling her name softly.

"Sadia, in the name of Allah, stop this crying."

"My child is no more," she screamed and held on to his caftan so tightly that he felt her nails dig deep into his flesh.

If he felt the pains reach his brains, he made no sound. He had to be strong if she was showing such weakness. He calmed her after much effort and rushed out to inform a few people to help take the child to the cemetery for burial. The sun was shining so intensely because the sky was clear and bright. It was like living a dream. Who could believe that just some hours ago, one could not see his own palms. "Allah is indeed great," he said in a whisper. As he walked towards Mal. Hashimu's house, he saw people on the street still busy clearing rubble or dismantling roofing zincs that had been blown over neighbours' houses or cutting off tree trunks that had fallen on houses or valuables or had simply, blocked roads. Seeing the damages the storm had done to the street, Saleh thanked God repeatedly that he did not have to undergo this form of calamity in addition to his loss. He walked without knowing where it was he was actually going. At a time like that, he cursed his fate that he was born alone to inch through this life, painfully bearing the bitterness of lonesomeness. He could not consider his sister at a time like that. He needed to have had some brothers, one at the very least. He wiped away the tears that rolled down his cheeks. He felt his stomach rumble and he knew that he had not eaten anything since the day broke. How could anyone think of food in the face of such calamity? he wondered. He decided to go to the houses of some of his customers who, sometimes, passed time on the bench in front of his kiosk. He thought of Kaana, a middle-aged Kanuri man whom he could call his closest friend. The problem was Kaana's house was at Mairi Village, a settlement that was neighbour to the University of Maiduguri, some twenty-five kilometres away from Pompomari. He decided against going that far and retraced his steps back to his immediate neighbourhood. His first port of call was Mal. Hashimu's house. The man Hashimu sympathized with him and joined him in calling on four other men who quickly provided the *likafani* (piece of white cloth used for burial) and soon, they were at the graveyard because in spite of their personal woes, death always required a complete change of plans.

Back home, some women had heard of the death of the child and a few sympathizers began to walk into the house to console Sadia and the other children. They sat with her on a large mat spread on the verandah while the children where shooed to the smaller room used by the girls. It was customary for sympathizers to remain in the house of the bereaved until the men returned from the graveyard. Hajara, Mal. Hashimu's wife, began reciting prayers for solace to the family of the bereaved and all the other women temporarily ended their small talks on the calamity of the day. Women were always excited for little opportunities of marriage, naming ceremonies and in the unfortunate instance of death to commune with one another and say their minds since they were almost always at home, seeing to the welfare of their families. When the prayers were said, a dark-skinned woman of about fifty-five whom most could not identify but who thankfully kept lamenting, "Ni Adama, eeyar Shatu" meaning "Ho! I Adama, the daughter of Shetu" and most of the women simply responded with heavy sighs "Hmmmm" because everyone of them, had something to say of the storm.

"You could hide inside your house when a heavy rain threatens, but this kind of calamity lifts the house and leaves you standing face to face with black fury," she said in Hausa and all the women, including Sadia, agreed with her.

"How is the old woman?" Hajara asked, looking at Sadia.

"I can't say what happened to her," replied Sadia who suddenly remembered that she had not even asked Saleh about his mother.

"We took her to the hospital this morning on our way to treat my son's cut."

"Her mother is also ill?" asked a woman.

"No, we took her unconscious mother-in-law to the hospital after the storm today."

"Allahu Akabar!" shouted many.

"May Allah spare her life," Adama said and all answered "Amin."

When the men returned from the graveyard, the women began to take their leave one after the other until the room became empty except for Hajara who remained seated next to Sadia. She constantly consoled her neighbour and reminded her that Allah (SWT) had ordained everyone's life and as believers, Muslims had to remain faithful in whatever circumstance they found themselves. They heard footsteps and Saleh walked into the room looking dirty and worn out. He greeted his neighbour's wife solemnly and listened to her words of condolence. He thanked her profusely and prayed for protection for her own family. She crouched to one side to give some privacy to the couple to converse. She did not want to leave just then because Sadia had no one else to stay with her.

"May Allah console you, Sadia," he said as he squatted before his wife.

"Amin summa Amin," she responded as the tears began to trail her face again.

Hajara could not help but notice the happenings between the two. Like Sadia, she too began to weep at what she felt could have been her lot. Saleh fought hard to control his own emotions in the presence of Hajara, he controlled his tears and quickly left the room. He had told the men who had left their personal woes to accompany him to the graveyard to go back to put their homes in order, as he did not see any need for them to sit outside, as was customary. He also visualized that he had to go back to the hospital to see to his mother's condition. The men went away with heavy hearts after offering their condolences to Saleh.

When they had all departed, he walked into the compound and the boys ran to him but he shooed them away and went straight into his room. He sat on the edge of the small bed for a while and gazed through the window. He was not sure he saw anything tangible except his thoughts that kept expounding his troubles for the day. He rubbed his forehead and the sound of the Imam, calling for the A'zar prayer, drifted into his consciousness and he let out a heavy sigh as he wondered how, in spite of the calamity that had befallen the town, the muezzin must continue with his duties to his brethren. He learnt an immediate lesson. Life had to continue in spite of all that had happened. He decided to join his menfolk in the prayers at the mosque rather than pray at home. He felt a sudden need to give thanks to God for His mercies; and above all, to ask Him to provide their needs and spare his mother's life. He was soon hurrying in the midst of men, who also seemed in a hurry, to respond to that particular call for prayers. It was a roll call of a kind for men of the neighbourhood, and whatever was left of their lives.

Saleh returned and, again, sat on the wooden bed in the room he shared with Sadia. His hands were cupped under his chin. He was in deep thought. In front of him was an old metal box. Such boxes were common amongst young secondary students of the

71

70s and 80s. This one had seen better days and had, perhaps, gone through many owners. The box was open and in it were cellophane bags of different colours. He sighed and reached for one of the bags and began unknotting it. He dipped his right hand into the bag and brought out some crinkled naira notes. After a little pause, he poured the entire content of the bag onto the bed. He began straightening them into their denominations of 1000 naira notes to the least 5 naira notes. He needed to make up the sum of 50,000 naira for his mother's bill. The money in the bag had been for that month's purchase for the store. Now, he needed to not only make up the sum but also, look for a way of restocking his store. He counted the money painstakingly. In all, he got 27,230 naira; a little, above half of what he actually needed to make the required sum. He did not know where to go for help. He thought of his fellow shop owners like Koji whose shop was at the next bend to his. He would go to him for help. As he made up his mind to go to Koji, he began to pack the cellophane bags back into the old box. Without informing Sadia or even taking notice of the children in the compound, he made his way out of the compound as briskly as he could manage. He walked along the crowded street without looking into the faces of the people that passed him by. When he was at the front of his own shop, he noticed that he had not locked the door. He was suddenly alarmed and he went for the door. When he stepped into the kiosk, he did not notice anything except the fact that sand had covered the entire stock. He thanked his luck that no one noticed the opened door, otherwise, the shop would have been vandalized to add to his myriad of woes. He picked the padlocks and stepped out to secure them on the door when he noticed the fallen branch behind the shop. It had affected the back end of his shop but did not undermine the roof. He had no time to attend to that just then so he went on his way to see Koji. As he walked the single bend, he saw people still hurrying along to solve one problem or the other. Some of them, he was certain, were visiting sites to evaluate the extent of damage that other people had suffered. At the turn, his body suddenly caught the chills. He stood transfixed on the spot for what befell his eyes left his mouth agape. Koji's shop had been uprooted by the storm. Sympathizers were everywhere helping him to assemble his scattered wares. The roof had been blown off and was lying unconcerned at a distance. Saleh did not know what to make of his fate. In the midst of the people, he saw Koji dragging a large bag of rice or beans, he could not immediately tell from where he stood. When he had recollected himself, he walked to Koji with an outstretched hand. The two stood there, holding hands in a handshake that told a long, sad story of their many years of struggle in the business. He stood there pondering the calamity that had befallen them all. He could not certainly voice what took him there and so, after much commiseration with his partner, he begged to leave. As he walked along the crowded lanes again, he wondered where he could go for help out of the urgent need that he was faced with. He thought of going to his friend, Kaana, but within the time left for him, he did not think that he could make it to Mairi just then. He kept walking and thinking about the tenacious dilemma that was his. In his mind's eye, he saw his mother lying on that hospital bed, motionless and helpless. He was all her hope, all that she could rely on. His elder sister, Maimuna, was married to the head butcher in Madagali and the man was better off left to deal with his own teeming family members with two wives and maybe twenty-eight or more children. He must have enough problems of his own. Saleh walked on without knowing where he was heading. The sun was still hot. The trees that braved the storm stood still and would not even flicker their leaves. They had had more than they had bargained for. People were busy removing tree trunks or branches from their rooftops and children were scattered all around the streets, the playing ones were kicking a rounded makeshift ball made from some old rags. Some of the children were helping with clearing the debris. Saleh walked on like someone on an inspection visit to the town. He was not like a person in a trance, he was conscious of his environment even though he did not know his final destination. He was just going to continue to walk until an idea of someone who could help him out of his dilemma could come to his mind. As much as he did not want to voice the thought of Mal. Zubairu, that remained the visible helper in sight. He would not go to the man for anything he convinced himself and walked on. It was nearly 4 pm when he looked at his wristwatch whose strap could roll up to his elbow. It was surprising how he was able to wear it without it ever falling off. He stopped at some point and made to turn back but something urged him on and he walked till he was not far from Kaana's area. He realized that he had covered a great deal of distance in that aimless walking meant only to provide him with the opportunity to think. The distance to Kaana's place was less than the one he had covered. In the realization, he quickened his pace and prayed inwardly that he would meet his friend in less a calamity than the one he was faced with. When he arrived Mairi, he went to Kaana's house because he did not expect him to go to the market after the morning storm. His friend was standing with another man when Saleh greeted solemnly. Kaana was surprised to see him and without being told, he knew that something was amiss. He quickly ended his talk with the other man and literally pulled Saleh towards his house. Saleh was happy to see that his friend was not affected by the storm. They exchanged greetings, Saleh told his firend about the effects of the storm on his family. He told Kaana about the dead child, Usman. He informed him of the fact that he came to see him directly, from the graveyard and how his mother was lying between life and death at the ICU unit at the hospital. Kaana was visibly shaken by the news and he condoled with his friend and prayed that the old woman recovered her consciousness.

"I must say that I am very lucky," said Kaana after some silence that befell them.

"Indeed, you are very lucky, my dear friend. You need to see the devastation in Pompomari. Some people lost their roofs, for others the storm brought down walls and for others it was tree trunks that fell on their houses or other properties like cars, shops, just mention it."

"In that case, it was mild here."

"Naturally, Pompomari is at the end of the town from the north, whereas, you in Mairi here are almost at the centre of town. Imagine the distance the storm had to travel to come here. The effects had waned by the time it got here," finished Saleh in a very solemn voice.

"God is indeed miraculous," said Kaana as he too became silent. "So, what are you going to do about Mama's indisposition?" They were close friends and had since their childhood grown used to calling each other's mothers by the name

"Mama".

"Actually, I came to see you over the matter. I was wondering if you could help me with some money to complete her hospital bill," he said turning to face his friend.

Kaana was lucky. He sold seasonal perishable goods and did not need to stock his store at any given time. Often, he sold out his wares by the end of each day and bought new stocks in the morning. At times such as the one at hand, he had cleared out his stock of tomatoes, spinach, onions and the likes. When he visited his site that morning, he had only to pick his table and bench from a little distance where the storm had dropped them.

"What can I do to help?"

"The hospital requires fifty thousand to keep her at the ICU, I don't have the whole sum and I need you to help me out with the balance."

"What is the balance?"

"I have twenty-seven and need a balance of twenty-three thousand."

"23,000," he said silently. "When do you need it?" he added and scratched his head pondering on the situation that his friend was facing.

"In less than an hour, Kaana, you can't believe that I walked to this place on foot. I did not know what I was doing; I was just walking until my legs brought me to your doors."

"I will give the sum to you," he said after a while. Saleh could not thank him enough.

"She is also my mother, come in, come," he said and stood up to go into the inner part of the house.

Saleh followed his friend and Kaana went straight towards his wife, Bintu's room. When she saw him, she was alarmed because he rarely visited them due to the nature of his business. They exchanged greetings. Kaana quickly told her what happened and she was visibly saddened. She promised to visit Sadia the next day and to see the old woman in the hospital too. They went into another room, apart from the bed and a little black and white television, the room was empty. Amongst some clothes hanging on a wooden hanger on the wall, Kaana dipped his right hand into one of them and brought out a bundle. He sat on the bed and began counting the money. Saleh watched him as he counted out the 23,000 and then handed it to him. With both hands, Saleh received the money and showered blessings on his friend. Soon they were on their way to the hospital since Kaana insisted on seeing the old woman and Sadia immediately. Saleh's happiness was immense.

The Hospital

Maimuna lifted the old woman to a sitting position because she needed to feed her. Like her mother, Maimuna was fat. She had borne seven children for her husband, the head butcher in Madagali. The bus driver, Mallam Mustapha Direba, who travelled the route to Mubi, told her about her mother's condition. It was three weeks since the storm and the old woman had been moved from the ICU to the female medical ward, an open ward that was crowded with women with varied medical needs. When the pressure was much, Saleh had sent for his elder sister to come and be with their mother because Sadia was not able, any longer, to cope with being at home to do the cooking and then coming back to stay with the old woman until Saleh closed from the shop in the evenings. They had held on for a week and could no longer, unless Habiba was to stay out of school to help at home with the cooking. Saleh hated the last option, as he did not want anything to come between his daughter and her education, so he had sent for his sister. With Maimuna around, he could even sleep at home and things became a little easier to manage.

The old woman was fed only *kunu*, a syrupy gruel from millet flour. She would ladle a little at a time into the constricted mouth of the sick woman slowly like a mother feeding a disagreeable child. Maimuna was doing a good job of it because Sadia could never lift her up all by herself without calling on some other women next to their bed to help her out. Regularly, she would feed her mother and clean her with a wet towel. The doctors gave the old woman a 50/50 chance at any relapse. She was to be managed properly to prevent that from happening. Although she was fully conscious, she was unable to speak. She would labour and what came out would remain inaudible. When her grandchildren came in over the weekend to see her, Ahmed had wondered why she was drooling. Ummi had pinched his side to shut him up, that was not the usual scenario known to them.

The boy had looked up at her and resigned his fate, not understanding the look on her face except that it was stern. Sadia wondered in her heart what the old woman might have thought at them seeing her so indisposed as they did. She could swear that a cauldron was churning within that placidity that everyone saw. Sadia knew better than take that look for granted. She was going to perform her duties as was expected of her.

The old woman had to be taken out twice a day for physiotherapy at yet another ward. After feeding her, Maimuna wheeled the chair to the physiotherapy section. It was a tasking exercise because the old woman was always uncooperative. Getting her to mount the wheelchair was yet another uphill task that needed some extra hands, which was in short supply. The hospital was still in short supply of staff although the emergency that greeted the storm had minimized, patients still outnumbered the attendants and doctors. Therefore, with the help of just one person, often the next bed patient attendant, Maimuna got around getting the old woman onto her wheelchair. What she did was to push the chair close to the bed, collapse the arm nearer to the bed and legs first; she would incline the old woman's buttocks and gradually slide her nearer to the seat until the bulk of the woman slid into the space. During all of these, the old woman would position herself as though she was getting set for a fight. She would emit a hiss-like sound from the right side of her mouth that could still function. She was complaining about something she did not like in the movement. Maimuna would always marvel at her mother who could do nothing for herself and yet not be satisfied with any help that was rendered willingly. Thus was their morning and evening routines and when they made their trips to massage her limp sides, the woman attending to their next bed neighbours would wonder silently at the disagreeable nature of the old woman and then thank God that she herself was not saddled with her care. It was okay that she was asked only now and again to help which she did because Maimuna herself was such a cheerful person. Maimuna would wheel her mother to the heat panel and with the help of the two staff in attendance, move her to the flat bed where some hanging flannels of heat would be lowered on that part of her that was limp and thus, she would be heated up as it were until she winched from pain. Miamuna herself would stand at a distance, watching in silence. Sometimes she felt sorry for her when it seemed that she would forget and attempt to will her useless arm to function but when the reluctant limp would not respond, a tear would roll down her right eye. Maimuna would also wipe away her own tears and look away.

In the evenings when Saleh came to see his mother, he would bring with him their food. For Maimuna, he would bring what the family was having for supper and for the old woman, he would take broths of whatever he could afford. His shop was far from doing well. His burden had increased with drug prescriptions that he had to purchase and with the markets not too good, he could barely keep his head up.

On one of the evenings, he walked into the ward and saw Mal. Zubairu sitting with his back to the entrance. He said some greetings which was not directed at anyone in particular. The man answered spontaneously and wondered why Saleh had not thought it wise to inform him that the old woman was in the hospital. He offered some lame apologies of having too many things on his mind. He moved closer to his sister and whispered something into her ears. She stood up and went to the bundle that he placed on the side cupboard. She loosened it and brought out the Samira dish, which he said had his mother's meal. He looked away from the woman on the bed because he did not want to see her searching communicative eyes. Mal. Zubairu saw all that was going on and made to leave.

"I wish you Allah's mercies," he said and dipped his right hand into his pocket and placed a large bundle of money under the old woman's pillow.

"I will come back to see you," he added, looking towards the woman for he knew that although she could not respond to his words, she could hear every word that he said. She was his ally.

"May Allah refill your coffers several times over," said Maimuna to him as he made his way out of their presence. Saleh barely said an audible gratitude to the man. He felt so little that he was compelled to accept Mal. Zubairu's charity in that formal way. The old woman saw it all and still wished inwardly, that a rich man like Zubairu would be an asset to a family like theirs.

Maimuna fished out the bundle of one thousand naira notes

from under her mother's pillow and began counting with excitement. She could not believe herself when the money would not end as she counted each note between shaky fingers and setting them aside in 10s. When she got 10 sets of ten thousand naira, she gave a low gasp, "₦100, 000," so that the people around them would not hear. Saleh had looked away all the time as she counted the money and sharply turned to face her when she exclaimed the final figure. The look on his face was that of shock and disbelief.

"₦100,000," he said to himself with a deep breath and looked at his clenched hands. He did not know if he was happy or sad. ₦100,000, why would he part with such a large amount of money? he wondered and concluded that it was all towards the grand plan that he had plotted with his mother. He did not know if he should touch the money or tell his sister to do with it as she pleased. He felt like crying some bitter tears. He felt Mal. Zubairu gave so much to humiliate him. He was being baited.

He stood up, his facial expression revealed anger that was also painful to carry within. Anger and want struggled for supremacy. The storm had broken him and he was a desperate man with mounting responsibilities, yet in his heart was a turmoil that he could not handle. Maimuna was shocked at his sudden change and she reckoned that Saleh surely must have a brawl with Mal. Zubairu, which she was curious about knowing.

"Oh, Saleh! Look, look at the handiwork of God in our lives. Only yesterday, you were not sure where the money for the next medicine would come and now we have more than enough." Maimuna kept on rambling over the windfall; she obviously had never counted so much money before. Her attitude further aggravated his anger and he felt helpless and had to walk out of the ward without another word to her.

Back in his room, he sat on the edge of the bed and reflected on the event at the hospital. He wondered who might have told Mal. Zubairu that his mother was in the hospital. He was bent on knowing how the man had to know about his mother. When Sadia sent Ahmed to call his father to have his meal, Saleh sent the boy back to fetch his mother. Sadia looked worried as she entered the room. She sat on the tip of the bed, a position from where she could see his face in full.

"What is the problem?" she asked thinking the old woman's condition had deteriorated for the worse.

"Did Mal. Zubairu come here to the house recently?" he queried without wasting any time. He looked Sadia straight in the face as he awaited her answer.

"Yes, he …"

"What? Sadia, I never knew you were a hopeless woman until now!" His anger garnered a new flare.

"Why? What for?" She was obviously confused about his choice of words. What could have gone wrong with Mal. Zubairu coming to the house? She was going to tell him that the man came in the morning when he, Saleh, was at the shop. What time had she to tell him when he came in to pick the food for the hospital and he was only just returning. She gaped at him, fuming and boiling for reasons best known to him. She could say nothing at a time like that so she walked out of the room and left him there, standing and screaming at the wrong persons. He did not eat his food that night. He kept thinking of the brutal fate that was going to befall his family should he succumb to the craftiness of Mal. Zubairu. True, he needed the money now that his mother was in the hospital and his shop was not doing well. He still had Kaana's ₦23, 000 to pay back although Kaana had never for once referred to the money and would not stop making his wife cook food for the patient and her keeper in the hospital. He was all the brothers that Saleh could never have.

In the morning, he hurried into the ward to find his mother not on her bed and Maimuna not there. His heart gave a leap and began racing as blood rushed to his brain. He felt a terrifying headache grip his temple and his eyes were unseeing suddenly. His legs grew weak and he held on to the metal rung of the bed and in a voice that was only a little more than a whisper, asked, "Where is my mother?" The question was directed at the patient on the bed next to his mother's. The woman's caregiver was covered up and perhaps, sleeping on a mat on the floor when she heard Saleh's fainting voice. She recognized him then greeted him with a smile.

"They went for the heating."

Immediately a surge of happiness bathed his body and he was flushed with what seemed like new life. He had thought that his mother had succumbed in the hours of the night. He thanked her and sat on the chair by the bed to wait for them. He hoped that they would not take long in coming because it was not visiting hours yet, as he had just told the guards that he had some food to deliver to his patient.

When he was seated, he asked after the health of the woman on the bed next to his mother's and her attendant, who was fully awake, answered in the positive.

As he watched people moving about the ward, he realized that he was in a female ward and felt a little uncomfortable as the young women were hurriedly covering their exposed heads or other parts of their bodies on seeing him seated there. He himself suddenly became uncomfortable and as he was showing the basket he had taken there to the woman, Maimuna wheeled his mother back.

"Ha! Saleh good you are here to give me a hand."

Saleh looked at his mother while his sister kept on about the helping hand that seemed to worry her so much. If he had not come, was she not going to solicit some other people's help? Anyway, he pulled the chair and with a little support from Maimuna, whisked the old woman onto her bed. He placed his mother's head on the pillow and turned to go when Maimuna called after him.

"Saaaleh! The money, what are we to do with it? You left yesterday and did not even touch it."

He stopped without turning to face her. When she had finished, he told her to send ₦23,000 to Kaana Shettima and keep the rest for the old woman's medicines and then walked out of the ward without waiting to hear her approval or otherwise.

"How do I reach Kaanaaa ...?"she shouted after him and was sure, he heard her all right.

Saleh walked on like someone haunted by a mortal fear of people's faces. With his face downcast, he walked to the bus stop and boarded an already steaming bus that needed two more passengers to fill. He sat on a wooden seat called attachment, which was actually an additional seat constructed by the owners of the buses to increase their passenger capacity and as a result, earn more fare. The result was often a terrible congestion and the suffocating mixture of sweat and dirt combined to deprive some passengers the liberty of access to clean air. The bus soon began creaking along the narrow roads, swerving here and there to avoid potholes and at other times, falling inadvertently into some that were scattered on the expanse of the road to Pompomari. Saleh got off along a lateritic path close to his shop. The place was deserted and as he opened the doors, his mind went back to the questions he heard his sister ask him a while ago. What sort of response was that anyway? he asked himself. He saw himself as a hypocrite who could not swallow his pride and accept the hand of assistance from Mal. Zubairu without much ado about the issue with Habiba. Was his not touching the money physically exonerating him from the use of the money? If he ordered the money to be used for his mother's medicines, did that not mean he had a part in the way it was spent? Could he ever convince people close to him that he had nothing to do with the money? What was it anyway that bothered him so? Was he a failure by the single misfortune of the storm which compelled him to accept charity from a man as irresponsible as Mal. Zubairu? Yes, that was what the man was. He was his father's contemporary by the simple reason that they did business together. No doubt, his father mentored him as though he was his own son. It was wrong for Mal. Zubairu to desire a child young enough to be his granddaughter. So many questions lay unanswered in his mind as he gazed into the distant horizon beyond optical recognition. The sun was already out and he needed to send someone to tell Kaana to go for his money.

꡴| Madagali |ꡳ

Three weeks had passed since Maimuna's arrival in Maiduguri to care for her mother in the hospital. In all of these weeks, she had never gone to Saleh's house for once. Her baths and feeding were all in the hospital next to her mother whose condition had remarkably improved in the period of her being around her. The old woman still drooled but her understanding of what went on around her had improved. She accepted her broth and *kunu* with flaccidity as before, perhaps because the taste of what she was fed remained practically the same every day.

Maimuna packed their dirty clothes and went to the bathroom to have them washed. She had done their washing twice every week since her arrival at the hospital. When she saw her mother close her eyes in sleep, she decided to go to the washing tub by the bathroom. It was a little after eleven in the morning and the sun was up high in the sky, the kind of weather that was kind to laundrymen. As she washed, she hummed an old song that young girls sang during their coming of age initiations in Shaffa, her father's hometown, where they had lived before moving to Maiduguri. That was then of course, young girls did not undergo initiations today. There had been mass campaigns by NGOs like BOCODEP, GLOBAL RIGHTS, NEEDS and others like them that preached against the major focus of the rite, circumcision. She tried in her head to remember some details about the rite but all she could see was some remote period during the healing of her wounds. She was never one with a good memory. Some people believed that she suffered some kind of loose memory after a particular childbirth that was protracted. Whatever it was that she suffered, she did not see a doctor over it because as local dwellers, many things were left to chance and afflictions like that were almost, always attributed to the will of God. When she went back to the ward, she met Saleh and her son waiting for her, Saleh was on the only chair meant for visitors while her son,

Adamu sat on the mat on the floor. Their expressionless faces did not reveal a thing to her. Saleh looked away each time, avoiding her eyes. She exclaimed in happiness and kept the bucket and detergent under the bed.

"Adamu, how are you and everyone else back home? When did you arrive?" she asked all questions without waiting for the boy to respond. The boy Adamu, perhaps in the neighbourhood of 23 years, did not also want to meet his mother's eyes. He could not also confront his mother with what took him to Maiduguri, at least, not with his uncle seated there. He kept his head downcast.

"Maimuna, sit down," it was Saleh that spoke and his voice was so strange she could swear she had never heard him speak in that tone. She looked at both of them, one a brother, the other a son. They were her family. Suddenly, she feared that something grave had happened. The sudden arrival of her son coupled with the fact that he did not say he would come in the course of her stay in Maiduguri.

"What is it? You could at least tell me if my children are sick or something has happened to them," she was still looking from one to the other. Adamu's head was still down.

Saleh looked first at his helpless mother lying still and hoped that she was sleeping. He would not want her to partake in the bad news that had befallen them and so, he said in a whisper, "Your children are well my sister, all of them."

"Then who is dead?"

"Baban Adamu, is very ill and they need you to return immediately," Baban Adamu meaning Adamu's father since the boy was her first child.

On hearing that, she hauled herself on her son, pulling at his caftan and screaming.

"He is dead; I know he is dead, Adamu. He was well when I left him, how could he just die like that in my absence?"

When Saleh did not counter the fact that he was dead, she knew that it was over. They did not just want her back to nurse her husband, it was to go and begin *thakaba*, the three months compulsory mourning period for Muslim women whose husbands are deceased. She turned around to look at her mother but the old woman slept on. The sick woman on the other bed sat up while her attendant walked and held Maimuna by the shoulder. They were all weeping. The two women wept more for themselves and the irony that was life. Maimuna came to nurse her ill mother whom no one imagined could have lived that long and it was her healthy husband back home that had to die. Saleh wept, too, for his sister and more for whatever life they were to be reduced to with her departure. The woman consoled her with words that were meant to strengthen her faith and help her handle her loss. As all of these were going on, the sick woman on the bed kept wiping her tears and looking at Maimuna. Whatever she was thinking of, she did not voice except that it was obvious that she was in deep sorrow, perhaps of a personal kind. On the main bed, the old woman continued to lay motionless as though entombed already. She was still sleeping, and was probably not aware of the goings-on by her bedside. Maimuna stood there looking at her and the tears began to flow anew. She was thinking about her mother and how she was likely never going to see her again. She turned around and began to pack her things into an old bag whose zip had gone bad. Saleh and Adamu watched her from the corners of their eyes.

"What now?" she asked looking towards Saleh when she had put her things into the bag.

"We cannot leave Mother here all by herself. I suggest that Adamu stays with her while I take you to the park and then go home to fetch Sadia to stay with her. I had no time to make the arrangement, when I heard the news we came here directly."

"He is supposed to return to Madagali with me."

"I will come with him in time for the third day prayers tomorrow afternoon."

"Okay." With that she bade goodbye to the two women she had grown accustomed to for weeks. The attending woman walked with her to the front door and all the time, she reminded her of the hand of God in all that people do on earth. At the door, they hugged and parted. The woman stood there and watched Maimuna's upright head, until they disappeared at a bend. She felt sorry for her and imagined the miseries that would characterize her life on reaching home. Outside the hospital, Saleh waved a taxi, which took them to the park. At the park, Maimuna handed him something wrapped in a black cellophane bag.

"What is this?"

"That's the remaining money from Mal. Zubairu," she told him without looking at his face.

He held the money and said nothing afterwards. When they got to a bus conductor, he paid for her fare from his own money he had carried along for the purpose. He bade her goodbye and begged her to accept what had happened as the will of Allah. As he walked away, tears came to her eyes again and other passengers on the bus watched the two in silence. The bus took off after a few more passengers boarded. As usual, they were overloaded and Madagali, being two and half to three hours drive from Maiduguri, it was a raw deal.

The bus was silent for most of the journey and Maimuna was thankful for she wanted some inner peace to reflect over what had just been placed on her lap, and the uncertainties of what to expect on reaching home. She looked through the opened window of the bus and watched as the turfs of bushes flew past as they sped along the Maiduguri-Bama road. The road was probably built in the seventies during the military regime of General Olusegun Obasanjo and the Udoji windfall from oil that greeted the Nigerian people then. That was when the government was still interested in providing public utilities for its people. The Civil War had been fought, lessons were learnt, and with the memories of the colonial masters not long gone, corruption was not as large-scaled as was the case today. Her mind again travelled to her home in Madagali, she wondered what her husband's younger wife, Aisha, was feeling. Their husband, Hashimu, for that was his real name, kept the two of them each in her own section with two rooms, a latrine and cooking space for each woman. She had seven children, and being his first wife there was an extra room for the grown boys, Adamu, Salisu and Bomai at the entrance to the house called, *zaure*. The second wife had four children, all boys. Suddenly, fright caught her and she realized that she had four daughters and was therefore likely to have less inheritance than Aisha and her sons. She was visibly alarmed and shifted on her seat. The bus was probably moving at 120km/h but it was not fast enough for her. She looked over her shoulders at some of the people in the bus, most of them were dozing with heads drooping, and she was alone in the great hurry to arrive

Madagali.

The bus arrived Gwoza and as it was leaving the town, a loud sound broke the regular rhythm of the tires on the hot, tarred road. The driver pulled to one side of the road and came around to have a look at the tire. It was flat and all the passengers disembarked so that a replacement could be fixed. It was about ten minutes drive from that point to Madagali motor park. Maimuna was beside herself with anxiety, as she had to come down like other passengers. From where she stood, she could see the top of the roof of the first filling station that lined the road as one came into the small town. She contemplated walking the remaining distance but chose to wait like all the others. When she got down at the park, she took a bike ride popularly called *achabba*, to her home. As they neared the compound, she saw a number of people seated on mats outside the house. She got off the bike at some distance of 50 metres or more from the men gathered outside. She rearranged her veil to ensure that her body was properly covered and again, began to cry on nearing them. They were so many people of all trades and businesses that had come to pay their last respect to her husband who was the head butcher of the town. He was an indigene and had married and brought her to live in his hometown. She held tight to the bag in her hand and walked through the crowd of people at the front door. Bomai saw her first, he told his brother and, together, they followed her as she got into the house. Inside the house was yet another group of people, only this time, they were women. There was screaming and yelling going on all at the same time. She went to her own section of the big house and all the women began to cry with renewed zest at the sight of her. She threw the bag down and embraced her daughters as they rushed to her. Her husband had obviously been buried before her arrival.

"Zainab, what happened, what happened to him?" she was asking her 14-year-old daughter to whom she had left the charge of her own section. Her 17-year-old daughter, Rakiya, who was married out the previous year, lived with her husband in Mubi. She too was there pushing her very pregnant self towards her mother. Maimuna saw the protruding stomach through her tears and wept the more. The sight made every woman present to cry afresh, feeling sorry that Hashimu was not going to see his first grandchild. News went to Aisha's section that the first wife had returned from Maiduguri and those who wanted to pay their condolence to her began to walk into her room amidst the roaring cries of many women. Older women present pleaded with Maimuna to comport herself, as it was best to pray for him instead of the shedding of tears. By the end of the day, she and her children were sufficiently calmed and they continued to receive both men and women sympathizers. Foods were brought in from neighbours and friends' houses and mourners who decided to stay the night had enough to eat and drink. It was the culture and Hashimu was the head of the butchers, so, meat was sufficient.

Salisu and Bomai sat outside next to their father's younger brother, Abdullahi, and received all the condolences, there were still a number of men seated on the mat with them. Some men at a distance discussed other issues like weather and how the lack of rains was sure to affect their crops. Others discussed local politics of who to take the position of chief butcher in the town. In the misdt of all of these, people who did not hear of the death earlier still continued to visit the family. Abdullahi turned to Salisu, the older of the two boy and asked what arrangement they were planning for the three days prayers. He needed to ask them because they were no longer children and, therefore, had to have a say in their father's final farewell.

"Adamu will be here early tomorrow morning with Kawu Saleh," Bomai told his paternal uncle." *Kawu* means uncle but on the maternal side while *Bappa* is an uncle from the father's side.

"Okay, it will be best to wait for their arrival in the morning?" he was asking the boys' opinion.

"We can begin our own plans, Bappa, it is you who can say what is required because we do not know any of those things," Salisu said.

"We would need some cartons of sweets, biscuits and kola nuts. I can get some sacks of the kola nuts, say five bags, but they may not be enough. I know that some people would contribute some of these items that we have mentioned."

"Today is Monday and the three days prayer will be Wednesday, Bappa, let Adamu come tomorrow then we can conclude the plans," Salisu submitted.

They all agreed to wait till the next day to ascertain those things that they would need to buy which people were not likely to present to them. The sun was setting and the men outside began to depart after saying some prayers for the dead. Soon it was night and the compound had a sudden hush as everyone was left to his or her thoughts. The compound was a large one. On the entrance was a *zaure* which led to a narrow passage opening finally inside the compound. On the right, was Maimuna's section and on the left, Aisha's. At the far end of the yard was a cattle stead containing nine bulls. Next to that was a small pen with eighteen sheep and seven goats. All of which belonged to Hashimu's fattening regime. He would fatten them and then sell them to butchers. A good business for it fetched some good money that augmented his meat retailing at the abattoir. The women kept chickens, sold them for their little needs, and did not have to make little demands from their husband. The left side of the compound was Aisha's and her boys owned a little stall inside the house and sold some items like matches, Maggi cubes, salt and other household odds that people within the neighbourhood would need now and again without having to go to the market, which was far removed from their area. Aisha, a very enterprising woman, was able to always restock her wares and keep aside her profit. She did not need to use her money much, considering that she did not have daughters whose demands were more than what those of boys were. For herself, she was satisfied with whatever her husband gave her and since they were both in purdah, they did not go out much and, therefore, did not need many clothes. She was actually content with her life as a second wife to such a man as Hashimu who was well-respected in the society. He was a good husband to his wives. He provided for his family in ways that made his home the envy of most. He did not believe that Western education as a whole had any worth much less female education. He had always had serious conflicts with his brother-in-law, Saleh, whose views were at total variance with his.

In the morning of the next day, again the immediate members of the deceased family and some close friends of his sat on the mat outside the house to continue the mourning sessions. Food was brought to them on trays and a number of men gathered around the three trays and ate. It was believed that some people targeted moments like that and soon after the meals were had, they smoothly disappeared and resurfaced when they imagined that trays would be brought out again.

Inside the house, Maimuna held herself upright and was learning to live with the lot that had become hers and her children's. She was sitting in a corner and around her were women from the neighbourhood. They were the only friends that she knew and they had all been there for each other and had over the years celebrated and wept with one another. They had become like family especially the five women— Rabi, Hajara, Hauwa, Salamatu and Mamu. They were women of about the same age and shared their secrets without anyone outside of the group ever hearing about them. When Hashimu had married Aisha, they had been there for her and without having met the new bride, each one of them had hated the girl; even before they had the chance to meet her for the first time. Since then, they had had nothing to do with her because they all belonged to the first wife kind of club. They were all first wives to their husbands and one after the other, they had all been brought second wives and in the case of Hauwa, two other wives were brought in by her husband in quick succession of thirteen months between the second and third wives. These women felt the pains of the other so personally that it felt real. Maimuna was the first to lose her husband. Rightly, therefore, it was a moment of personal reflection for all of them. It could have been anyone of the five, considering the fact that Hashimu did not complain of anything before going to bed the night he died. He had been in his room, which was situated behind the animal stead, from the far right side of the compound. His one-bedroom kind of apartment adjoined the wall, led to the *zaure* from the west, and had another route leading to the main compound so that he could come into the compound without having to go out to re-enter from the main door. It was built in such a way that each woman could go into his room without the other knowing unless if she was looking out for an encounter of some sort. Aisha had found him still in bed and thinking he had overslept, had made to wake him when she noticed his half-opened mouth. She had never seen him open his mouth while in sleep in the eleven years that she had been married to him. When realization had dawned on her, she screamed the kind of screams that was half-human and half-animal. It was awful; she envied her senior mate who did not have to live with the sight. Maimuna's friends were not impressed by the endless account of the story on the discovery of their friend's late husband. They wondered, if the storyteller was thinking of a deserved award after all, considering that the *Tenant*, as they were wont to call all their second and third wives, kept recapping the account in dramatic and flavoured versions each time. Mamu took a tray of rice and stew to where Maimuna sat and the five of them sat around it. Maimuna was not ready to eat; she did not feel hungry since the news of Hashimu's death. They coaxed her to take a few mouthfuls which she did reluctantly.

Saleh and Adamu arrived the house at about eleven in the morning. They squatted before Abdullahi and the boys in condolence just as tradition demands, then turned to the other men seated on the mat. As they walked towards Maimuna's section, Saleh noticed some changes in the house. The section where Aisha lived had not been built at the time. He had only been there once, a long time ago when Maimuna had her first child, Adamu, who was the young man by his side. Twenty-three years ago, he reckoned as he was led to his sister's room. He himself was a young man then, probably 16 years old and not yet married to Kande, his first wife. Face to face with his sister, Saleh squatted and extended his arms in prayers. Everyone present extended their own arms before their faces and when he was done, he spoke words of condolences to her and her friends. Adamu imitated all that he did just as the women expressed their condolence in turn. Maimuna asked after their mother and if she was aware of her husband's death. Saleh had not told his mother for fear that the news could complicate her condition.

They rejoined the men outside and without any time wasted,

Abdullahi called them all to the *zaure* where they planned the three days prayers. They squatted on their heels and then Abdullahi placed the sum of ₦20, 000 before them on the sandy floor. Saleh looked at his feet and felt embarrassed that he could not hand in anything by way of contribution for Hashimu's burial. He began to apologize but was stopped by Adamu who knew his uncle's financial situation back in Maiduguri. In the one day that he stayed with Saleh, he had seen for himself that his source of livelihood, the shop, was a gaping space of emptiness. The old woman's illness had taken its toll on him. In that event, Abdullahi ordered the boys Salisu and Bomai to get some of the required items. One of the bulls was to be slaughtered for the day. As the day went, sympathizers began to make their own contributions and at the end of the day, they discovered that but for the bull, they needed not to have spent a single kobo of their own. The butchers association sent in the sum of ₦100, 000 and other cash donations that amounted to the tune of ₦380, 000 was counted, this did not include gifts of bags of rice, bags of kola nuts, and cartons of sweets, biscuits and so on which were in surplus. At the end of the third day prayer, the sum of ₦ 187, 000 was handed to Adamu. Saleh bade his goodbyes to everyone and was in the next available bus back to Maiduguri to face his own kind of tragedy, the management of his family life and the comfort of his mother in the hospital.

The Old Woman

It was seven weeks and three days since Maimuna went back to Madagali to mourn her husband. The old woman was more conscious of her environment than ever before. The regime at the hospital was tough for Saleh and more so, for Sadia who absorbed all the stress without complaint though there was a strange pallor that showed on her face and in every step that she took when she walked, her muscles went flacid. She had never really been a fat woman, plump or anything like that but her thinness in those few weeks had a sickly note to it. She seemed transmogrified into someone else that had no semblance to her old self. In all of these, she felt responsible to her duties as wife, mother and daughter-in-law to the sick woman who was difficult to satisfy even in her muteness. Saleh did his best; in the day, he was at the shop to make ends meet and at night, he would sleep at the hospital while she went to the house to be with the children. He had no time to see the transformation in her, or if he did, he said nothing. Habiba had to stop school and as he figured, just for the period that his mother was still in hospital and they needed someone to do the cooking at home while Sadia stayed with the old woman. The other children except Ummi, continued with school without feeling any difference. Ummi was the next in line to take charge of the problems of her siblings in school in the absence of Habiba. She was sad that her sister who loved school like none of the others had to be the one to sacrifice her lessons to keep the home. For the seven weeks that Habiba had to give up school, she had made it a point of duty to collect notebooks from Habiba's seatmate, Mojimola Taiwo, a Yoruba girl from the western part of the country. Moji as everyone called her would hand Ummi all the day's notes and beg her to tell her sister how much she missed her. At home, Habiba would quickly cook the meals and in between waiting for the water to boil and soups to simmer, she would pick Moji's notebook and copy the day's work into hers. As she copied, she would commit important points to memory. That way, she was able to satisfy her big appetite for books and keep in touch with the daily schoolwork that her absence caused her.

On a Thursday morning, Sadia had arrived at the hospital with the old woman's breakfast and was about to begin feeding her when she saw a drab mark on the top sheet on which the sick woman laid. She moved nearer to take a closer look and it was then that she realized that the old woman had soiled her sheets. That had never happened in the many weeks that she had been caring for her. She always beckoned on her whenever she wanted to move her bowels and with the help of the pampers that Saleh brought, cleaning her was a little easy as she only had to fold it from beneath her and pull out instead of washing the entire bedspread. From the sheets, Sadia's eyes fell on the woman's face and she noticed a strange yellowing on her forehead and around her collapsed cheeks. Her complexion had changed from its dark pigments to a strange jaundiced colour and it was frightening. Sadia did not know if Saleh had noticed the change in his mother before he left that morning or if the change was just making its appearance.

She bent her head and whispered in the woman's ears as she had often done, there was no response and she could not tell if indeed, she could understand her. Sadia looked at the patient on the next bed to her mother-in-law; the patient was a young woman of about 15 years who leaked urine from her private parts. They had learnt that she was afflicted by the non-stop urination because she was too young to undergo the trauma of labouring for babies. Her husband had abandoned her, or so they said. The young woman was on her bed and her catheter dangling down into a plastic *poo* container, under her bed. The word *poo* now refers to the container, usually plastic, on which children too young to sit on the regular WC could use for the purpose of defecation. Sadia watched her with anxiety in her eyes and knew that she could not get any kind of help from the woman. She looked at the old woman again and noticed that she was quivering in a slow kind of way and had some foamy substance at the corners of her mouth. Sadia dropped the plate she had been holding and ran to the nurses' station as fast as she could manage.

"Please, come quickly, come because something is happening to my mother." Without any word, a nurse stood up and followed her. When they arrived at the bed, the old woman was visibly convulsing and stretching every possible part of her body in an unnatural way. Sadia began to cry out as the nurse held on to the woman's arms and chest. She made attempts as though to compress the eruption that was brewing inside of the sick woman without luck. By that time, other nurses came with stethoscopes, and other medical tools that Sadia could not immediately identify.

"Wheel the bed to the oxygen room," cried a senior nurse to the two others standing over the bed. In seconds, the bed was on a fast race out of the ward and Sadia ran after them, tears running down her cheeks just as other people, patients and caregivers alerted by the emergency, watched as the hospital bed rushed through the crowded corridors. For a short while, they forgot their own problems and wished that the old woman would recover from the effects of the disaster that befell the town. As she ran after them, Sadia pushed through people who, oblivious of the running wheel, bumped into them now and again. When they got to the oxygen room, the nurses fixed the tubes as fast as they could around the woman's face and turned the knob releasing the lifesaver into the already impacted lungs of the old woman. She gave a good fight as she struggled with the little strength still entrapped in her soul. Sadia saw with amazement, the old woman's lust for life becoming stronger in the proximity of death. It was too late and soon as they had begun, the senior nurse announced, "We have lost her" in a voice that was unearthly to Sadia's ears. Afterwards, she simply stood there with unhearing ears and could not say what happened next. She woke up with a splitting headache and she was lying on one of the hospital beds in the nurses' station. It was unclear to her how it had all happened. She remembered in her head that she had heard something in the neighbourhood of death.

"Please, God, not again," she said silently as she awaited the nurses to look her way and see that she had regained consciousness. She began to remember exactly the scenario before she passed out. Was it possible that the old woman could die? she wondered in her head. It was not a believable thing to her because all through these several months of hospitalization, Sadia had come to visualize the woman as invincible. She had, in fact, always thought that death could not come near a woman as strong as her mother-in-law. The nurses not realizing that she had regained consciousness were discussing the incident.

"What a pity," said one of them.

"To lose your mother after several months of suffering."

"The woman was her mother-in-law," corrected another.

"What about the husband then?"

"His shift is in the evenings. She is the only one who can fetch him and until she herself is conscious, we can only wait for her to come through."

As all of the discussions were going on, Sadia had no idea of what she was going to do next. Was she to go and tell Saleh? Was she to wait for him to come back in the hope of staying the night with his mother before discovering that she was no more? She was so confused and finally decided to jump down from the high bed.

"Ha! You have come back?" one of the nurses said.

"Yes," Sadia did not know what else to say as she wiped the tears from her eyes. They all sympathized with her and asked if she could go to tell her husband. On hearing that, Sadia slumped to the floor and began to wail aloud.

"How can I be the one to tell him of his mother's death, please, help me? Help me, please." The nurses looked at one another and did not know what to say to her.

"Where do you live?"

"Pompomari." The tears would not stop. One of them murmured something to the nurse sitting next to her and then she looked at Sadia with pity in her eye.

"Where can your husband be found?"

"In his shop, the second shop, on the right as you get to the taxi park." It was 11.00 am in the morning and the nurse was to close from her morning shift at 2.00 pm, they asked her if it was wise to wait that long while the woman laid dead. In the end, she was convinced to go and tell her husband herself. Sadia could not explain how she got to Pompomari or how her legs carried her to the shop where she saw Saleh busy selling some items to some young children. Some men were seated on the bench in front of the shop; she imagined that they could be his friends. She walked past them without saying a word. It was easy because they did not know her. As she moved closer to her husband, the moment he saw her face, he was alarmed thinking that she needed some money for some drugs or some other things that the hospital might want for his mother. His wildest imaginations did not expect to hear what she eventually had to tell him. She had walked into the shop without attracting the attention of the men seated outside. Her face bathed in tears under the veil was not obvious to anyone but Saleh. He walked to her and held her right hand under the raised wooden support that made the shop window seem like one was standing on a balcony.

"Sadia, what is it that could not wait till I come in the evening?"

"Waiyo Allah na," she exclaimed in Hausa and collapsed on the floor of the shop before his feet.

"What do they want? You left Mama alone in the hospital, just like that! Haba Sadia."

"She is gone," she said in a whisper between convulsive tears.

He was silent. He had heard her words all right. The words hit him like thunder and he had to hold on to the wooden door for support as he found himself on the only stool in the shop which he used when he was tired of standing and customers were far in between. He held his head in his hands and thoughts of his mother as a strong survivor kept ravaging his mind and he almost did not believe her, except for the fact that Sadia did not joke about serious matters. She could not come to him to create a scene if it were not true. He recollected himself and held her up to her feet.

"Wipe your tears. God gives and he takes," he said solemnly, resigning to fate. In his heart, he wondered about the kind of calamities that had greeted his existence in the past months. He began to close the shutters of his shop without another word. Sadia, waited for him outside and would not look towards the direction of the men. The men wondered where Saleh was going to at midday, to warrant closing his shop like that. When he rejoined her outside, he excused himself and walked to where the men sat and told them as calmly as he could. They stood up and left whatever they were talking about and told him they were going with him to the hospital, and so they all went into a bus that took them to the University of Maiduguri Teaching Hospital. As they sat in the bus, they said kind words about life and death and quoted verses from the Qur'an to the couple to alleviate their pains.

At the morgue, Saleh stood still when the attendant pulled the handle to one of the doors, his heart beginning to beat faster again and when he lifted the cover from his mother's face, his hands quivered so much that he had to control an urgent desire to collapse and weep on the bare floor. Her face was contorted and ashy. He had the impression that she suffered at the last moment of life's extinction. It was not an easy sight for him considering the fact that he had passed the night with her and had seen her few hours before it had all been over. If only he had known that he was never going to see her alive, he might not have left her side for a moment. He loved his mother very much and he had really, never had the opportunity to say sorry to her since that night she refused to eat. It had all happened so fast. They had woken the next morning with that terrible storm that had been the reason for all his woes in life. His son, Usman had died in the storm and now, his mother who, in fact, had been literally dead since that same day. He attempted to recollect the last words she spoke on that day of hunger strike but could not. Two of his friends, Amadu and Garba, walked in with a *makkara*, a traditional stretcher used for the conveyance of the dead to its final resting place. Saleh was grateful for their presence and they helped to carry the *makkara* to a waiting pick-up van, hired by the other two men, Terab and Muhammadu, for the homeward transportation of the woman's body. Sadia went into the ward to pack their belongings. When she walked in, she knew that the news had reached everyone; patients and attendants alike. Those of them that could stand on their feet walked over to her and offered their condolences, while the others that were unable to simply sat on their beds whining, almost completely despondent in a way that seemed more depicting of self-pity. Some of them

99

even had tears on their faces as they helped her pack into three bags, what was then, her belongings. Before leaving the hospital, Sadia went to the nurses' station and thanked the three nurses for their help. It was about 2.00 pm when she walked out of the hospital gate to a taxi whose driver beckoned on her.

A large gathering of people, mostly men, were already seated outside her home. She caught sight of Mal. Zubairu sitting on the mat. His near mummified face etched at different points like an unfinished design on a slate. She could immediately tell that he too was in a deep shock. She pushed her way through the maddening crowd and was in the house only to face yet another kind of gathering. Women from far and near were already seated on mats that had been brought out from every room in the house and some from the neighbours. She began to cry at the sight of so many people who had all left whatever they were doing to come and pay their last respect to the woman that was known by everyone on the street and beyond as Maman Saleh Mai Kanti.

Some elderly women were in the bathroom washing the dead body of the old woman. Women and children were crying from every corner of the house. Habiba and her younger ones were also crying and Talatu, in particular, was tearing at her wrapper inconsolably. They were all going to miss their grandmother. Sadia wept for the woman from the deepest part of her soul. She knew that they had their own problems but overall, everyone of them would miss the old woman. Death was after all, a leveler and people tend to forgive and forget wrongs done to them the moment they know that their offenders were gone and never coming back.

The *makkara* was brought out of the bathroom and placed at the centre of the house. That was too much for everyone in the compound. Women began to wail and wriggle in genuine pains as their voices reached the men gathered outside and then they knew that the body had been dressed and ready for its final journey to the cemetery. At that material time, some men came into the house and left with the *makkara* and its content. The mournful cries assumed a high pitch and when it seemed like they had wept all their tears, the house began to be quiet. The first day of any death was always the worst because it was on the first day that bereaved people went into shock and unbelief. From the second day on, reality dawns on the survivors afterwards, life continues as acceptance takes over and histories are made.

৩|| Changes ||৩

It was 10.00 am. Saleh sat in the room looking into the distance through the holes in the curtains. He could hear the children's voices as they played in the compound. He had not opened his shop for three days because there was little or nothing left in the shop. Sadia was seated on a brown mat at another corner in the room, Talatu was lying by her side shivering with fever. They had forced her to swallow the home remedy made from leaves of mangoes, guavas, oranges and a handful of acacia flowers. The sweat built on her forehead and Sadia knew that her daughter was going to recover since that was the common belief. Saleh could not take the child to the hospital because he had no money to pay the bills. They had silently prayed for her. It had been difficult for him since the storm. Things had worsened so suddenly that at some points he had doubted in his heart if, indeed, prayers were answerable. He grew up believing that prayers said in time of hardship and desperation were, often, quickly answered. Since the storm, his lot had been very out of hand and there was not a 'functional' prayer that he had left unsaid. Moreover, how and why exactly he continued to suffer, and drag his family down in it, he could not explain.

Sadia continued to sit there, thinking her own thoughts, which were probably not far removed from Saleh's worries; the crumbling financial situation. Outside, Habiba, sat on the verandah, adjoining the old woman's room; thinking about school, which they had all missed for some days. Her only happiness was the fact that she had written the Common Entrance Examinations a week after the old woman's death. She was so glad that it turned out that way otherwise she would have missed it if the exams had been scheduled for earlier. Ummi was by her side, also thinking but about something else, food, and the fact that they did not have much of it in the house as before. The girls were hungry and so were the boys holding up and playing in the compound with their friends. In the last three days, Saleh had gone out early in the mornings and returned in the evenings without anything except dry cassava grit called *gari*. Ordinarily, *gari* was not their staple, especially when cooked in hot water and called, *teiba*. *Gari,* soaked in cold water and taken with some sugar, was a favourite snack to most people although, only when one had a full belly.

The old woman had been dead four weeks already. The debts that Saleh owed were numerous and he had no way of offsetting them without any capital at his disposal to fall back on. The kind people of the area had contributed to him which made his mother's burial a success. Mal. Zubairu for one had given him the sum of ₦50, 000 and other people had sent in their help in tens, fives and whatever it was that they felt could help him and which they could spare. He had friends but they were all low earners and although they had fantastic large hearts, they had little to share with others like him. He was still grateful to them all. During those days, he had remembered the Madagali people, and how they had supported Hashimu's family during the burial. The village people he concluded were better at communal support than the people who lived in the cities. Unlike the Madagali experience, at the end of the whole prayer days, money was returned to the bereaved family, his was not the case. Mal. Zubairu's money helped him in no small way. He was even grateful that he knew a man like that because when his mother died, his shop was not doing well and left alone, he may not have been able to afford the bills. That would have been a shame on his entire family.

As he sat gazing, he did not know from where their next meal would come. He kept thinking of asking Mal. Zubairu for help but something inside of him kept objecting. What was he to do? He was more confused than ever as he listened to the voices of the children echoing back to him. They were all hungry he could tell. As he sat in the room contemplating where to go for help, his divided mind said Zubairu while the other, Kaana. Although Kaana's first loan was paid in full, he had based on that good will, taken another ₦25,000 which Kaana wrote off at the death of the old woman. How could he run to such a man again? Besides, Kaana was only a vegetable seller who lived a day at a time. He decided against Kaana. It had to be Mal. Zubairu; it was a difficult decision but he had to save his family from starvation.

It was immediately after the *Mahgrib* prayers when Saleh took the last bend leading to Mal. Zubairu's house. From the distance, he saw Mal. Zubairu's frontage and four to five figures seated on the mat. He walked to some respectable distance and then stopped because he realized that they were eating. He did not want to barge in on them in the middle of their meal although, he himself had not had anything to eat. Sadia was able to cook some of the guinea corn gruel that his friend, Kaana, had sent to the house. He could not wait to eat with the boys back home as his need to see Mal. Zubairu was more urgent. He was fine as long as the children found something to eat. As he waited for Mal. Zubairu to finish his meal, he wondered just how long he could go on without food himself. He could not remember how long it was since Sadia had had something descent to cook. He wiped the tears that came to his eyes as he approached the men when he was sure they were through with their meal. The tray was discarded to one side and they all stretched themselves out to discuss politics and other related matters of interest to them. He approached the men with caution.

"Asalama alaikum," he greeted.

"Wa alaikum salam."

He went closer and shook the extended hands of all the other men and Mal. Zubairu's was last. It was only when he was next to the older man did he know it was Saleh. His heart missed a beat because he knew that Saleh had come to dislike him since he had shown interest in his daughter. He could not blame Saleh though, for wanting to protect his child even though religion did not prohibit an older man from marrying a younger woman. The greetings all done with, Mal. Zubairu wondered what it was that had taken Saleh to his house because, it appeared that he was not in a hurry to take his leave and yet would not say why he was there, perhaps because of the three other company that he had. After what seem like eternity for Saleh, the men, one after the other, took their leave after realizing that Saleh was not ready to divulge what brought him in their presence. The men were after all, Mal. Zubairu's friends and were probably, aware of his proposal to Saleh's daughter.

"You are welcome," said Mal. Zubairu in Hausa when the men had all left.

"Thank you, I hope your family is well?" he uttered demurely rubbing his palms.

"Alhamdulilahi, and how are you coping?"

Saleh knew he meant after his mother's death. At that moment, he felt the need to thank the man for his support when his mother was in the hospital and his invaluable assistance when she eventually died.

"Well, we thank God that we are still alive and healthy. I have come to thank you for everything that you have done for my family, I am sorry I could not come earlier."

"How is your business doing?" he asked as if he had not heard what Saleh said. Saleh was taken aback as he did not know how to answer that question.

"Ehmm … well, not so well," he could not say more than just that. Mal Zubairu watched him from the flicker of light coming from the electric bulb behind them. The pride in the man before him was still able to disconcert his calmness.

"What do you mean, Mal. Saleh?"

Saleh knew he had little time to afford to push the real reason for his being there. "I was wondering if I could get some loan from you, Mal. Zubairu."

The man did not say a word at first. He was silent as if he was reviewing what he had heard and if indeed, his visitor had said what his ears captured. Saleh too waited and the silence was a little embarrassing to him. He thought that Mal. Zubairu would jump at the slightest opportunity to help, if only to make peace and foster a lasting relationship between them.

"How much do you want?"

"Maybe, ₦600,000."

"₦600,000" he repeated, almost to himself as he looked into the distance at some secret images that were visible only to his own eyes. Saleh peered at him enigmatically in the half-lit night.

"I will give you the money, come tomorrow at this same time."

"Thank you, Mal. Zubairu," Saleh was anxious as he said the

words. The man simply waved his two hands, dismissing him in a breath.

"Tomorrow, come."

"I will come and may Allah continue to provide for you and your family." Saying that, he walked away as cautiously as he had done before. He did not just feel like walking home that night, not after his meeting with Mal. Zubairu. As he walked along the street on the other side of the lane that led to his house, he wondered about the *toshi* that was still lying untouched in his mother's room, ever since that night. Could he possibly, still want to marry the little girl, Habiba? He was scared of the whole thing and wished that he had not plunged himself deeper in his indebtedness to Mal. Zubairu.

When he walked into the house, the children had all gone to sleep but Sadia was waiting on the verandah to their room. She heard that usual feet dragging on the floor as it approached her and she was excited at the sight of him.

"Sadia, how is the girl?" he asked.

"Oh, she sleeps."

Saleh was glad to hear that. He did not want any more problems because, he felt he had paid his dues first with his son, Usman's death then his brother-in-law, Hashimu and then his mother, all of them, within a space of 4 months. Sadia brought him a bowl containing the *kunu* that the household drank for the evening. As he drank the gruel, he made plans in his head of how he would quickly restock his shop and return Mal. Zubairu's loan in good time and how he would be on his own feet again.

The next evening, just as he promised, Mal. Zubairu handed Saleh the money. Saleh was full of gratitude to the man and promised to repay him as soon as he could, which in his view, was not going to be long. The older man was happy with himself and told Saleh to solve his family problems first as he would not want to know that they were experiencing some handicap over money. He even inferred that he could go the extra mile for the old woman's family because she was good to him. Saleh hoped that the inference did not extend to his mother's handling of Habiba's case.

In the morning of the next day, Saleh woke early with a cheerful air and walked to the market to purchase items for his shop. A pick-up van delivered some assortment of goods to the shop and that day, he began selling goods to some of his old customers, who on their way to Koji's shop, stoppped over when they saw that his shop was open. He greeted each customer warmly and arranged his two benches outside where his old friends would again begin to gather. That day, he sent a boy, with some food items to his house. He was quite hopeful that he would manage the money from Mal. Zubairu to uplift himself from the destitute position he was in.

Sadia was gobsmacked and her mouth could not work at the sight of the contents of the three bags the boy brought in to her. She asked and queried to be sure it was actually meant for her. She called Habiba and the other children to come to where she sat.

"Mama, what is it?" it was Ummi who got to her first. The boy turned around to see the approaching children and did not know what to make of it.

"See, seeee," she said opening the bag to show Habiba who was at hand to view the contents.

"Meat, rice, tomatoes ..." she stopped and turned to the boy asking, "Who sent you?"

"Mal. Saleh Mai Kanti, is this not his house?"

"Yes, it's his house. We only wanted to be sure that he sent you."

"He sent me," the boy said and began to walk towards the door to make his exit from the house.

"Baba," Sadia called to her son and ordered him to go to the shop and ask his father if he sent the boy with the items. The boy ran out towards the direction the errand boy was going.

In the house, Habiba told Ummi to get things out in readiness for the preparation of a real meal but Sadia stopped them, insisting that Baba Audu had to return with words first. They looked at each other when Baba Audu returned and instead of shouting the awaited joy from the main door, the boy walked to his mother. Everyone, including Sadia, was exasperated by his silence. They watched him as he walked to his mother, he was not conscious that what he had to say meant so much to everyone there, including himself.

"Father sent him."

There was a loud shout of joy from all of them and only Baba Audu did not quite understand the gravity of his message. Even Talatu and Ahmed who were sitting on the verandah shouted in happiness. In what seemed like minutes, the fire was made and meat was already simmering in a pot. Sadia also had something to do, as she too was anxious to get the food ready. Ummi even joked to Habiba that even the pots were happy because like them, they had not been greased.

Two months after the severe times suffered by Saleh and his family, he had not taken a single kobo to Mal. Zubairu. What he alone knew was that he did not only owe Mal. Zubairu but three other people, Garba ₦15,000, Illia ₦32,500 and Yakubu, ₦113,650. He had collected provisions from Yakubu to restock his shop when his mother was still in the hospital and because of the overwhelming cost of the drugs, he had not been able to save anything from the sales of the goods. From Illia, he had collected a loan of four tins of vegetable oil and a bag of flour and just like Yakubu's, the money went on hospital bills and drugs. His friend Garba, who helped him with the little arrangements at the old woman's death at the hospital, later on that day, loaned Saleh the sum of ₦30,000 to help him settle the hospital bills before the body of the old woman was released to them. He was so indebted to all of these men because it was they, who sheltered him from shame and humiliation.

When at the end of the day's sales, Saleh sat back in his shop to calculate the real amount that he owed, minus Mal. Zubairu's, he got the total sum of ₦159,150. He wondered how he was going to handle the payments of the three men. He counted the money from the day's sales, ₦4,211. He was going to save every day's sales and at the end of each week, he would take some part of his profit to one of the three men so that they could have a sense that the debt was being serviced, albeit, little at a time. He could not give them all because he needed to remove the capital money from the daily sales. That was how he had managed the shop in the past before the storm put an end to all he had. With that final decision, he walked back home and met everyone joyous and cheerful. As he sat down to have his own meal, which was set on the mat opposite the old woman's door, a new fear gripped him.

He realized that he was still to feed his family from those same daily sales. It was obvious, that even when he is able to pay his three other debts, Mal. Zubairu's would take him eternity to repay; it was after all, the working capital. Knowing Mal. Zubairu as he did, he knew his fears were not unfounded. He could not play with the serpent simply because its eyes were closed.

꧁ Mallam Zubairu ꧂

At the Gamboru market, along a range of stores sat four men. They were laughing at some jokes and eating roast meat, known as *suya,* from a large brown cement paper. Behind them, the sales-boy, Jibrin, was searching for change for the customer who had just paid for a set of a piece of 6 yards of Nichem Wax. The master, Mal. Zubairu, sat copiously on a Persian rug, chewing at the meat that he threw into his large mouth now and again. His head, dark and capless, shone from a recent hair shave. The *wanzam,* local barber, was an expert, and had been in charge of the head for over thirty years. The same *wanzam* took care of the shavings of his late mentor, Mal. Audu, Saleh's father, until his death. Mal. Zubairu was a very wealthy man who owned the entire row of about forty shops along the Gamboru market in Maiduguri. Apart from letting out some of his shops to other traders, he was a wholesaler who was into merchandise like brocades or *sheddah* materials, worn by men mostly, although women sometimes wore them. He was also a major distributor of Dangote products like sugar, semovita, rice and noodles. The textile shop was where he spent his day and only occasionally would he visit his other shops otherwise, his managers and accountant reported to him regularly. Some of his friends often went to the textile shop at Gamboru market to spend some time with him because they were sure that he was an avid eater of the peppered meat, *suya.*

He coughed slightly and called out to the boy, Jibrin.

"Kai, Jibrin!" he shouted in Hausa.

"Na'am Alhaji," replied the boy, calling his master with the male prefix 'Alhaji' used to refer to a rich man or someone who had been to Saudi Arabia to perform the holy pilgrimage, in Makkah. A rich woman who had also been to Makkah on a pilgrimage was called Alhajjia or simply, Hajjia.

"Get us some drinks." He turned around to ask his friends

what they would drink and when they all answered "The usual," he turned back to the boy and said, "You have heard them, now quick."

The boy picked four empty bottles from behind one of the shelves and rushed out. His master did not have to say what he was going to drink because the boy knew without being told. Before long, he set four bottles of cold drinks before them. The three friends had Coca Cola, while he took the only bottle of Sprite.

"As I was saying," said Mal. Zubairu, "I am taking a new wife very soon," he grinned from ear to ear.

"What? Who is the lucky woman?" one of the men, Waziri, asked.

"Alhajiii ..." said another, a mischievous smile playing on his face.

"Hahaha ..." Mal. Zubairu laughed and leaned forward and whispered, "You need to see her, a young shot," he laughed aloud to the applause of the others. The men began to whisper between them and eyed Mal. Zubairu as he adjusted his flowing gown on the rug. He shot out a short leg towards his guests and sat upright to the envy of his not-so-rich companions.

"When is the big event?" asked another called Bello and the others nodded, meaning they would all want to know the day and if possible who the woman was.

"No, my friends, I was only pulling your legs."

Saying that, he tried to change the topic but his friends knew him better than that. They knew he was not joking, he never joked over matters like that, in fact, they suspected that he had gone far with the matter than he was telling them. They secretly wished that he had looked at the direction of their own houses since they all had daughters that a man like Mal. Zubairu could be interested in marrying. Every father would be glad to have him as an in-law for then all his family problems would be taken over by the very rich Mal. Zubairu.

"Haba, Alhaji," cried Bello.

Mal. Zubairu studied them closely as each man spoke his mind on the issue. He was a crafty man that fed on the weak points of others. His feelers conveyed to him what he wanted to know, which was what his close associates would say should he take on yet another teenage bride. He felt a deep sense of satisfaction because the discussion though a trap, had a marvelous momentum that he needed to respond to in the same velocity as the pulsating power and desire burning inside him. He was set for the battle of the heart, if not the soul of the little angel that had occupied his heart since that first night that he saw her in the dim moonlight. He was lost in thoughts and his companions needed no further confirmation as to the intention of their host. Almost at the same time, they requested to take their leave of him perhaps to plan for the race for the rich man's purse. When they had departed, Mal. Zubairu smiled glibly to himself.

That night, as he was relaxing on a Turkish carpet placed on a large mat in front of his home, Mal. Zubairu received first, his accountant, Mr Khalid Kumar, an Indian, who came daily to present to him the ledgers from all the branches of his group of companies. Most times, the different managers met him there and had to wait because the CEO first attended to the final figures before looking at the breakdown in respect of each business. They exchanged greetings in Hausa because, fortunately, Mr Khalid Kumar was born in Kano State, and spoke fluent Hausa except for his Indian accent. They walked towards an outer room which Mal. Zubairu used as an office where he received and kept business documents which he himself could not read. He kept them all the same. They sat comfortably on formal office chairs and began looking into the book of accounts that held the secret to Mal. Zubairu's wealth. He was gaping at the pages and of course, he had to accept this, whatever the *bature* told him, *bature* meaning whiteman or any person of fair complexion.

Mr Kumar explained to him the accounts and what was deposited in the three banks that the businesses operated. He had always trusted the accountant even though people had reasons to suspect that the Indian was short-changing the group of companies because his boss could neither read nor write. At some points, he had been advised to introduce his sons to the financial running of the businesses. Knowing the trouble that he underwent with his sons, he preferred to keep the Indian even if it was true that he misappropriated some company funds. Illiterate as he was, Mal. Zubairu knew what he was doing when it came to his investments. When he heard footsteps at the door, he knew that the managers of his varied businesses were also outside, waiting to see him. He was a busy man by any standard.

What Mal. Zubairu did which people did not know was that he had a standing order with the three bank managers, to clarify with him before money was withdrawn from any of the accounts. He also made it almost impossible for the accountant to deposit less than he collected from the businesses since the money had to pass through a number of people who documented the in and out of products and their sales at all points. In addition to all of these, the firm, Sanyolu and Associates was an auditing firm that looked into his accounts. He had always believed that if in spite of all the steps taken, someone decided to embezzle his money, he would see it as the will of Allah.

When he was through with his staff, he went back to his carpet and ate his dinner with six of his younger sons ranging from 12 to 5 years of age. When they had finished, he sent the eldest to the house of a man called Bashir while the others took the trays into the house. Bashir was the mason he regularly consulted when he had any need to build or fix his house. The man came promptly and sat on the far end that was only the mat. He would not sit on the carpet because it would not be respectful for him to do that. They exchanged greetings and then Mal. Zubairu told him what he wanted him to do in the house.

"Bashir, you will start work on the rooms adjoining my section," he instructed the man in Hausa.

"Okay, when can I start, Alhaji?"

"First thing tomorrow morning."

"Okay, Alhaji."

"Let me know what materials you will need to complete the work. You can go in and make estimates."

The man left him and returned after a long while. He sat before Mal. Zubairu with a piece of paper in his hands.

"I have looked at the work, Alhaji."

"Eheen, how much?"

"Ten bags of cement, one trip of fine sand ..." He was cut short by his host.

"Bashir, tell me how much you need to complete the room and its parlour to be habitable, that's all I need from you, not wood or cement."

"₦185,000."

"I will not have you come back to me for more money."

"Okay, ₦200,000 then, Alhaji," said Bashir, a little stiffly and feeling trapped by the man he had always thought abhorred any form of contract addition by simply ignoring you and looking the other way as you speak. He knew he had to be careful before he got into trouble with the man.

"₦200,000 will do the work?"

"I think so, Alhaji."

"Don't think, be sure."

"It will do the work, Alhaji."

"Good, come tomorrow to Gamboru and take the money," he said and began to chew at a piece of kola nut he threw into his mouth.

The man left his side after bidding him a restful night. Mal. Zubairu sat there for a while before he retired to his section of the large house. That night, he did not sleep much as he thought out the plan to get the marriage to the girl, Habiba, contracted in a hurry. The completion of the building already contracted to Bashir was the first step towards that. In his head, he had every step spelt out and he knew just how and when to execute each.

In the morning, while still lying in bed, he thought about his son, Liman, 46 who lived at Gwange Ward, he wondered what he was up to since the death of his wife, Altine. In his head, a voice told him to relinquish the girl Habiba to Liman and he jumped up from his lying position as if the suggestion came from another voice in the room. "No!" he said to himself. "Everyone should look for his own happiness." His other son, Mohammed, 37, lived in Gombe as a fish merchant and from what he heard of the boy, he was into some good business. Sanusi, 36, was the youngest of his grown sons and from a different mother. Born to him by his second wife, Barira, who left him when the boy was only 6 years old. Sanusi chose to be an Islamic clergy who engaged in large-scale mixed farming and seemed satisfied with his vocation because he exploited the services of his Quranic pupils and had, therefore, very minimal expenditure at the end of the day. His farms thrived on the free labour rendered by the children sent from other parts of Northern Nigeria and sometimes, from Niger Republic, Tchad and the Cameroons. They were the *Almajirais* (pupils). Mal. Zubairu remembered how he had wanted all his sons to learn the white man's secret books but they had refused to complete formal education and had chosen marriage and whatever they did for a living. He had settled them in their own houses with reasonable capital to begin their own chosen life-styles. With his daughters, he had had no worries over the four older ones because he had married them off as soon as he got wind that they had begun seeing their monthly flows. How else could he be of value to them except to protect their honour through marriage? He had eleven other children, seven boys and four girls from his younger wives. Rabi, his second wife, had not borne him any child yet. In his life, he had been married to seven wives. He kept a total of four at any given time according to Islamic injunction. His first wife, Zuwaira, the mother of Liman and Mohammed, he had lost over twenty years ago while he had divorced the other three at separate times due to their strong-headedness. Now, he had three and needed to complete his home. He was a chronic lover of women. He loved each woman for her special qualities. Sometimes when he was sitting alone, he would reflect on the different reasons why he loved each woman and often, he had laughed to himself, calling himself the 'old fox'. He would smile mischievously when he revisited their thoughts in his head. First was Ramatu, a short buxom, middle-aged woman with a high shrill voice and blessed with large bosoms. He reminded himself of how she would wrap him between the cleavages and even offer him her milk and he had actually learnt to suck the nursing woman's breast. He would dream away, longing for the warmth therein. He believed that she herself found some relief in him sucking the milk because it was always too much for her babies who were born scrawny. The second, Rabi, was not so endowed. She had a smallish stature, was very dark and had wide nostrils, but the old woman, may Allah rest her sweet soul, told him that if ever a woman could mix condiments to delight a man, it was Rabi. Although he pitied her because he could tell that she made extra efforts to bleach her face to a lighter complexion because of Hauwau his third wife. He could tell that Hauwau's coming into the household had a lot to do with the mental imbalance that Rabi had been plunged into. He had never regretted marrying her though, because he made sure that it was only on her nights that he invited his friends to eat outside his front gate with him. She was an asset for the keeps. His third, Hauwau, very fair-skinned, was a woman meant for a king. Gazelle-like, she was a beautiful woman by any standard. Her curves were at their right places, nothing was out of its position, a perfect physical creation. In spite of her three children, she was a creature for worship. He never had enough of her and whenever she was sliding out of bed, he never tired to steal glances at her curves and smile with satisfaction, she was his invaluable asset. As for his new-found blossom, Mal. Zubairu reflected and grinned like a shy schoolchild at the thoughts of Habiba. To him, old age was something dreadful and a constant reminder of the fact that one was on the verge of expiration. To handle that, he needed a blossoming youth that he found in the girl, Habiba. The freshness of youth was to him, magical and as the saying goes, 'an old wine put in a new bottle,' was all that one needed to spice up one's life. His life would do with some rejuvenation that marrying Habiba promised.

Mal. Zubairu simply laid there, smiling to himself and how memorable he thought some of his experiences were. He was satisfied with life as it was since he had what he wanted out of it. Other things he was sure to get at a fee which, incidentally, included Saleh's pride in the fight for the possession of the girl, Habiba. His thoughts went to the long wait after the old woman's death. Moreover, no one mentioned the *toshi* that he had already sent showing his intention to marry the girl a year earlier. At moments like that, he wished that the old woman were still alive. How was he going to broach the matter to Saleh? He had pondered on the possibility of visiting him to talk about the issue but his will had always disappointed him. He would think about visiting Saleh to ask for the money, not because he needed it but for want of something to discuss or hinge his visit on, as always, his courage had failed him. He realized, however, that he had to do something eventually and, the sooner the best for all of them. Having so decided, he set a day to make his visit to Saleh's house.

ᐒ‖ The First Step ‖ᐔ

It was on one of those days in the month of December, when you woke to a morning that was misty and hazy at the same time. It was about 11.00 am in the morning and the sun was making an effort to undermine the haziness in the atmosphere without success. It was dry and cold and people were in high-necked sweaters and shawls to keep out the cold breeze. The trees were swaying gently to the rhythm of the sounds made by their leaves as the morning cold breeze blew through them subtly. It was 6 months after the storm and the rains had come and gone. The year was also winding to its end and the extreme dry and dusty harmattan wind that blows from the Sahara towards the western coast of Africa was at its peak. Mothers were particular about their young children and stuffed them up with extra clothing to keep them warm. During times like that, people's diets changed. More and more people drank hot beverages and *kunu* and ate more than was necessary to help them generate body heat. The zone usually experienced longer nights and shorter days during the harmattan months, which meant that their days began late and ended early.

Saleh had just then opened his shop to begin the day's business. He sold more products that were cold weather-friendly, like bottles of Vaseline Petroleum Jelly, sugar, Lipton Tea and other brands of teas. His life had returned to normal and his children were attending school regularly. The only hitch to his happiness was the debts that were not reducing as fast as he would have wanted. How could he really pay up when he had to feed his family from the profit? He walked a tightrope and constantly, he reviewed his precarious situation to know what choices were open to him and what compromises he could possibly make in the end. Always, he ended up with one resolution, to see to the payment of the other debts before Mal. Zubairu's. He did not know why he felt that way but he rationalized that Mal. Zubairu was never going to ask him for the money because of the respect that he had for his parents' memories. He saw him more like a member of the family so he would settle the outsiders first before the 'home debt', after all 'blood they say, is thicker than water'.

That evening, as the family sat eating their supper each at his own angle, they heard a voice at the main entrance voicing some greetings to the household.

"Wa alaikum Salam," replied Saleh who sat closest to the door. He looked into the darkness towards the *zaure* for the visitor to make his appearance. Saleh did not immediately recognize the figure that emerged until he was closer to him with an extended hand in greetings.

"Ah! Alhaji, it's you."

"Salam," he said again as he dropped on the mat with a heavy thud. From where she sat, Sadia recognized the man's voice. She was alarmed as to the real reason for the visit because she had never liked or trusted the man.

"You are welcome; I hope your family is well."

"Everyone is well, Alhamdulillahi, how about your own family?"

"We are surviving, join me, Alhaji, I was just making a start at my evening meal."

"Alhamdulillah, I am okay, thank you. I have come to discuss a very pressing matter but I can wait for you to finish your meal," he said and moved to a side.

"No! It is alright, Alhaji, I will listen to you first." Saleh pushed the tray of food to one side and turned to face his visitor. He did not provide any chance for the man to greet his family from across the compound though he knew that Mal. Zubairu would have wanted to say hello to Sadia and the children.

"Are you sure you would not finish your meal? I can wait really."

"No! I am fine, you know it is cold out here, I will like to listen to you first, and there is no problem at all."

"If you say so, but maybe we could step outside to talk about it?" suggested Mal. Zubairu.

"No problem," he turned to Sadia and told her he would be outside the house and he led the way with Mal. Zubairu closely at his feet. When they were outside, he turned to face his visitor.

"Yes, Alhaji."

"Ehmm ... Saleh, I came actually to discuss with you ehmm ... about ehmm ... you know, theee, theee ... ehmm, the things thattt I sent ehmm ... sometime ... ago," he continued stuttering in that manner and Saleh was in no mood to hurry him up. He watched the man, his arms folded around him. He had thought that the man had come to ask for his money but since he had taken a different dimension, he was going to be stern with him.

"Alhaji," he said reflexively, "I was not privy to that arrangement, I am sure you are well aware of that. It was between you and my mother and whatever she did with your things or where she had kept them, I do not know and I would appreciate it very much if you can keep me out of it, please. I thought that you really came to see me over something that was reasonable, like the money I borrowed from you but No! You will come over something as ridiculous as that."

"Did you say ridiculous, Saleh?"

Saleh was not interested in the discussion anymore and took a step towards the door but stopped and looked at Mal. Zubairu. "Just look at you, Alhaji, the girl you are talking about is younger than some of your grandchildren. How can you not see that she is too young for marriage and moreso, for someone as old as you?"

"Ah! Is that the bond you are contesting?"

"Leave my child alone; look elsewhere for your whims," then he walked towards the door and stopped suddenly when Mal. Zubairu's voice came to him in whips through the cold night air.

"If that is how you want it, Saleh, then I guess I have no alternative but to ask you for my money first thing tomorrow morning," he said and immediately turned around and walked to his car, parked across the street.

Saleh stopped suddenly, his heartbeat racing fast. Around him was a silence that stood detached and he felt naked. He placed his right palm on his forehead and he felt the sweat already formed. He was shivering in a cold December night. He turned in time to catch Mal. Zubairu's car driving off and he could swear he saw the old head gleam from the street lighting arranged along the street. He could not imagine what he had got himself into. Slowly, he walked into the house to meet Sadia's curious interrogation. She had sent the children into their rooms because it was too cold for them outside. Saleh did not want to talk about it with anyone, not even Sadia.

"What did he want?"

"It's nothing," he lied.

"I have never trusted that man. What did he really want?" Saleh said nothing in response all the while that she talked to him. When she was tired of just standing there, she walked quietly away. He sat there thinking about what Mal. Zubairu had just told him and he did not know what step he was to take in respect of the threat. He pushed his tray of food to one side and sat there wondering how it was that he even thought of Mal. Zubairu as family. He saw the man as bloodthirsty, *"If that is how you want it, Saleh, then I guess I have no alternative but to ask you for my money first thing tomorrow morning,"* he heard the man's voice snarl back at him. 'First thing tomorrow morning.' Where was he going to get ₦600,000 to give to the desecrated monster, that was bent on a nihilistic approach that disdained both morality and religion? It was the likes of Mal. Zubairu who painted a different picture of religion. Why did it have to be an old man like him anyway that had to marry his daughter? Did he not have sons who could be interested in Habiba? It would be easier to accept giving his child to a young man under the kind of pressure that he was in, not Mal. Zubairu and his ageing heart of over sixty years. What could he possibly offer the girl anyway? These thoughts bothered him and he was not able to sleep when he finally made it to his bed.

The next morning, Saleh woke up with a depressive and foreboding feeling all over. He could not look at Sadia in the face when she kept a breakfast tray before him. He asked after the children and was told they had all gone to school. He felt her loneliness as she sat at a corner in the room. Since the death of the little boy, Usman, and his mother, Sadia had slowly become withdrawn from most of those things that had made her happy in the past.

She walked like a zombie around the lonely house when everyone was out and on that day, as he ate his reheated meal of the previous day, he expected her to ask him the same question he had not responded to after Mal. Zubairu's visit the night before.

However, he was not dealing with the Sadia that he knew, she was a different person. He knew that one of the problems that she had was the fact that he had hardly been in the mood to lay beside her every night. For that reason, the coming of her cycle each month left her with a strange disposition, which only he knew what.

He could not blame himself for that because of the myriad troubles that he had been facing, not to talk of the one at hand. He decided not to tell her anything because he would want to make efforts first, to see that he took care of Mal. Zubairu's threat.

At the shop later that afternoon, he had few customers but some of his friends did come for some gossip, which he was not in the mood for. He excused himself and locked the shop because he wanted to see Kaana, who was like a brother and he needed to confide in someone. He paid the bus fare and got down close to where his friend sold his goods and walked the little distance.

"What happened?" Kaana asked him leaving the onions he was arranging on the table.

"I had to see you over something that just came up. It is urgent."

"Sadia and the children, are they well?"

"Everyone is well. Kaana, it is Mal. Zubairu again," he said in a voice that was ghostly.

"Ehen! What does he want, the money?" he quickly added. From the look on Saleh's face, he could tell that it had to be the money that he borrowed from the old man.

"The money and he wants it today. I am surprised he was not at my door this morning to ask for it."

"How come?"

Saleh then told him about the visit last night by Mal. Zubairu, and how he felt his last words were threatening. Kaana listened to him, his brows arched in sorrow. He did not like the sound of what he had just heard. His subordinates knew Mal. Zubairu for his callousness. He remembered a story that made the rounds some years back of a Yoruba taxi driver who scratched Mal. Zubairu's new Mercedes Benz 500 SL with his dilapidated, old model Ford. The taxi driver was said to have prostrated flat on the tarred road for the Alhaji to run over him with the Mercedes because he knew pleading could take him nowhere with the man. Mal. Zubairu had the man detained for about three days until other taxi drivers that were his kinsmen staged a public demonstration.

Kaana felt the chills come over him. How could they stand up against a man such as Mal. Zubairu? In fact, apart from the fact that Saleh owed the man, which in itself was an assortment of problems, the man was capable of framing up some staggering amount and claiming that Saleh owed him that.

"What is your plan?" he asked Saleh who was watching him all the time as he delved into the archives of rancid memory.

"I don't know what to do, Kaana. I have nothing to sell to raise the money. Besides, you know that I still owe Garba and others so much."

"The only solution that I see may be to play the game along, my brother."

"What is the game?" he asked with anxiety showing in his eyes and hoping that his friend would say something tangible to get him out of the mess.

"Let him have the child, Saleh." He was thrifty with words.

"What! Allow Mal. Zubairu take Habiba?"

He was astounded. His eyes instantly reddening, he stood up, walked a few paces and turned back to where Kaana sat, he opened his mouth to say something but no words came out and he collapsed on the ground. Kaana rushed to help him up just as another man who was witnessing all, also rushed to help. Saleh quickly regained his senses and sat quietly on a bench where he was placed. Suddenly, he felt ashamed of himself when he saw that he had attracted the attention of everyone close enough to see what took place. Without thinking, he stood up and before all the protesting voices could tell him to sit down, he himself staggered back on the bench, exhausted. He rubbed his forehead continually to cover his face from the people that were asking Kaana if he was sick. He lied that Saleh did not feel well. They sympathized with him and prayed Allah to relieve him from whatever illness he suffered. When they had all gone back to their businesses, Saleh wanted to go back home but his friend would not let him go back alone for fear that something could happen to him. Therefore, feeling imprisoned, he sat there only occasionally meeting the gazes of the men who showed him empathy.

Kaana did not wait for the usual time before packing up his wares for that day. As they walked towards the bus stop, he noticed that Saleh was better composed, although he would not say a word in response to his conversations. Saleh kept thinking of how he could agree to Kaana's suggestion. In his head, he knew that it was easier to succumb as his friend had suggested but he knew he could not live with the guilt. What would he be doing to a child that loved to acquire education? They got down at the bus stop next to his shop and walked the distance to Saleh's house.

Sadia and the children welcomed him and Habiba spread a large mat at the far end of the compound under a young Neem tree that was anxious to provide shade to the homestead. Kaana had stolen a furtive glance at the girl, Habiba, as she adjusted and readjusted the mat to meet her father's instructions. He did not know what his friend was worried about because the girl to him was old enough to be in a man's house. As they sat under the Neem tree, Saleh looked up at the tree's vibrant leaves and wondered how it was that Baba Audu and Ahmed were not so interested in mutilating that particular tree. It was approaching 3.00 pm, the two men sat there quietly at first. Kaana sipped from the *kwanon sha* (water dish) that Talatu had set before them, cleared his voice and turned to his friend.

"Saleh," he called, "you know that if I had the money you are looking for or had any property to sell, I would have readily given it to you. You know that, don't you?"

"Yes, it is so," replied Saleh, looking at some loose thread on the mat.

"Look at it this way, if you have a piece of land anywhere at all; let us put it up for sale. We cannot go to another person to loan money to pay another loan."

"How can I have a piece of land which you do not know about, Kaana?"

"No! Just in case you do have some inheritance which I might not have known of."

"You know that I have none."

"How much of the other debts have you settled?"

"I have not yet started repaying them."

"You have not started? When were you thinking of starting? When their own patience also runs out? You and I are sellers, I do not use up all my daily profits on feeding my family, Saleh. I thought we agreed that we were going to save from our daily sales?"

"Look at you, Kaana, you talk as if you don't know what I have been going through these past months. How could I have managed to cater for all the calamities that befell me one after another, heh?" As he said those words, he felt like breaking down and weeping but he knew that his family and especially, Sadia, was watching him from wherever she was hiding in the house. Although Kaana felt sorry for his friend, his own hands were tied.

"Give the girl to the man!" he whispered with lots of emphasis in his voice.

"Oh! Kaana, the girl is too young, can't you see?"

"Then pay the man his money and keep your girl! You cannot have your cake and eat it. You should not have gone to Mal. Zubairu of all people to borrow money, especially when you knew he had his eyes on your daughter. You were not thinking, Saleh, and when you were taking that decision, you did not even think of coming to me because you knew that I would not have allowed it. Now that you are in his trap, I strongly believe that playing along is the best security for your family. Open your eyes, Saleh, open your eyes!"

Sadia watched the men from her bedroom window. All the while as Kaana was lifting a finger or swaying an arm to explain as it were, a difficult mathematical theory to a dumb child, she focused her gaze on her husband's impervious face. After Mal. Zubairu's visit the night before, she was almost certain of the reason for the heated discussion between the two men in the compound. She wondered, however, if her husband was going to agree to Mal. Zubairu's demands. Personally, she was not sure where she belonged; was she for Habiba to go or stay on to complete her primary education? A year ago, the girl helped her with Usman and to divert and cushion the old woman's troubles, but with the two gone from her life forever, she did not know what she wanted for herself much less, for some other person.

Baba Audu approached the men with a plastic kettle containing water for ablution. It was way after the Al Asr prayer. Kaana waited for Saleh to join him then he saw the boys, Baba Audu and Ahmed, coming to join in the *Jamhi* (congregational prayer).

Kaana took his leave soon after the prayers and as Saleh walked beside him to the bus stop, he thanked him for coming. He did not go to his shop afterwards but went home to sit on the mat where he and Kaana had sat on. He was not in the mood to talk with anyone but when his sons came to sit with him on the mat, he was glad for the distraction that they provided.

After supper that day, Mal. Zubairu sent a hungry looking man to him. The man could not have been more than 28 years or thereabout. He met Saleh sitting on the mat and greeted him solemnly.

"Alhaji sent me to you."

"*Tau!* What did he say?"

"He said you were to give me a message for him."

"Tell him I will see him tomorrow," he said and looked away and the man left immediately.

Saleh had simply said that to dismiss the man not because he had decided on what step he was going to take tomorrow. As he sat, he again wondered at the options that were available to him and he would intermittently get stuck at what he thought was best for the girl, Habiba.

That night, he could not sleep again. He still could not face Sadia with his problems and she too did not ask. She knew that it would come to the open eventually.

A Decision

The cold wind stung right through the many layers of garment on everybody's back. It blew across the land, relentlessly picking the dry fine ashy dust and blowing it through closed windows and doors. The cold was more severe than most people could remember. Saleh was walking to his shop that early morning and he felt the wind bite through his skin. He could not understand the reason why he had refused to wear his sweater, his *danchiki* caftan was barely covering his shoulders leaving the arms empty of any form of covering. He came out that way because he did not see any reason for him to want to protect himself from whatever it was that the cold inflicted on people. What was the point pretending to be a man when, in fact, one was less so? He chastised himself now and again for his failure to protect his own family from shame and ruin. He believed that death was better than the disgrace that was hanging over his head and he had come out to open the shop to keep himself from weeping before his children or some of them, who he was about to betray.

When he opened the shop, he attended to customers that stopped by to pick one item or the other and all the while, he thought of what to tell Mal. Zubairu. He weighed Kaana's advice on the one hand, and his own personal convictions on the other hand, the picture remained grim. Kaana had asked him to think about the future of the family as a whole and not the attempt to safeguard one member. For most of the day, in his mind, he deliberated the options and as he walked to Mal. Zubairu's house that evening, he had reached what to him seemed rational and in the overall interest of all concerned. He figured that in a man's every action, a sacrifice or price had to be made or paid as it were. In his case, someone had to pay a price for the sake of the others. An inevitable price needed paying in the circumstance that he faced. Even in the rustic and rudimental exercise of feeding ourselves, some organism pays the ultimate price. So what

126

was his final decision on the issue? Did he need therefore to sacrifice one of his own for the others to survive? It is believed that when hunger pushes one to the abyss, that one is capable of feeding on his fellow men to survive, and where there is no other but oneself, one resorts to eating one's own flesh to keep the heart alive. These sorts of behavioural manifestations of man were often inexplicable, they were called, *survival of the wise*. Overnight, he had to learn the supreme lesson about existence and he was walking towards his tormentor's house to look him in the eyes and show him that he was a *survivor*. Yes, he had to eat of his own flesh to survive; that was what it was.

He stood at Mal. Zubairu's door and waited for the appearance of the man he had expected to meet sprawled on the Turkish carpet as he had often met him. When the man did not immediately show up, Saleh was impatient at the delay. After what seemed like eternity to him, the man finally made it outside, the gleaming head emerged through the door; Saleh wasted no time as he began delivering, as it were, a death sentence on himself. He saw himself, as someone on a mission to carry out a suicide bombing which meant his own end because betraying a child that he helped to bring to the world was, to him, akin to killing himself. In a reflex, he imagined what theosophical beliefs laid locked in the heart of a suicide bomber that were ethereal and higher than the material world where personal auras are perceived. A journey, they say, of a thousand miles, begins with a single step. Saleh had taken his first step to maturity and self-destruction whichever came first. With his own hands, he was destroying what he had built to satisfy his predator, Mal. Zubairu. With that, he turned to the man and said, "Take the child, but send her to school." He turned his back and began to walk away. He did not even flinch when he heard the voice of the old fox, calling desperately after him. His feet hurried on because the wheel of change had been steered and like the Domino, it was bound to crumble.

He walked through the *zaure* and re-emerged in the compound. It was a cold night, Sadia and the children had all gone into their different rooms to keep warm. Sadia was lying on the floor, on a three-inched stripped mattress. He could not tell if she was sleeping although it was too early to imagine that she was. He called her name all the same and as she stirred, she opened her eyes and saw a glimpse of his face from the little rays of light that shone from the lantern she had placed outside in case the children needed to go to the bathroom in the night. She was immediately alarmed at the glare in his eyes. She could swear that she had never seen her husband's face assume a jaundiced look as it did that day.

"What is the matter with you?" she queried and sat up, her wrapper tied over her bosom.

"Sadia," he began, going straight to the point, "a lot have been happening to me since the death of my mother. Actually, it all began with that same storm that took my son away and later on, killed my mother. Things went from bad to worse and today, I am heavily indebted to my creditors."

"Do not talk like that, Saleh, I know you are an honourable man and you can pay everyone of them whatever it is that you owe. Ask them to allow you some extra time." He noticed that she called him by name, which was something he had never heard her pronounce since their marriage.

"No, Sadia, it has gone beyond that. The others are okay but Mal. Zubairu will not reason with me and wants to go ahead with his marriage proposal, which he had arranged with my mother. He has given me no time at all. It is either I allow him take the girl for wife or I return his ₦600, 000. Today was the last day that he had given me to do that."

"What? And you were going through all of these and said nothing to me?" she was furious with him as with the situation at hand.

"What would you have done, weep your way to his house? No, Sadia, I do not blame him, it was my mother who started all this, and now, she is gone and has left me in a predicament that is swallowing me up."

"What have you decided to do then?"

"Decided to do? Did you hear me at all? Do I have an option here or you do not know who Mal. Zubairu is?"

"I never liked that man since the first day he set foot into this house. I knew that he was cooking up some bad news with Mama, God bless her soul."

Saleh looked at her and wondered how she could bless the

memories of a woman like that even when she was his mother. He hissed and regretted having taken his mother for granted in that respect. How could he have known that he was going to be plunged into a mess like the one he was faced with? He bit through his lower lip and when he heard Sadia say something, he turned to her and asked, "What?"

"I was wondering how you would break this kind of news to that girl. You know that she brought her Common Entrance result since two days now and I told her to wait and not tell you because I knew that you had too much on your mind lately; but I never knew it was something like this."

"Common Entrance?" Saleh held his head between his hands as the tears rolled down his cheeks. It was not until the next day that he summoned the courage to call Habiba to inform her of the impending arrangement. She picked her head veil and met him in the *zaure*. Her expectation was that he was going to send her somewhere outside the house. So as she walked good-humouredly towards the dark interior, Sadia knew, from where she stood in her room, that her husband was inside the dark interiors, waiting to have the most difficult encounter of his life.

"Baba, here I am, you want me to do something?"

He looked at her image in the dark hut and his eyes fell on his feet. He wondered how people began broaching difficult subjects like the one he was faced with even when darkness provided some cover.

"Habiba," he began, "I am your father, is that true?"

The girl was confused and hoped that she had not done something wrong to make her father talk in the way that he was doing.

"Father," she cried and moved towards him and fell at his feet. Her heart was beating fast and she thought that he was ill or something. "Father," she repeated, "please, what is the problem?"

"Habiba, I have accepted the proposal to give you out in marriage."

"Marriage?" It had to be a dream. She looked first at her father, her eyes accustomed to the dark hut then at the surrounding and then at him again. She pinched the back of her hand and looked at him again. "What kind of marriage?"

"You know about marriage, don't you?"

"No! How can I know about marriage now?"

"It is difficult, Habiba, you cannot understand. My hands are so tied and I had to give my consent."

"Consent to be married, Father! Now, what about my school? I want to go to school, please." She was still not sure she was not imagining or dreaming the encounter, she hoped that she would wake up and realize that it had all been a bad dream.

"I have already accepted, Habiba, you will go to school from your husband's house."

"I will what? Father, are you really serious about what you are saying?" She began to cry out aloud as if a bandit had attacked her. She screamed so hard that Ummi ran to the *zaure* to see what was happening to her sister. On seeing her father there, she stopped at the entrance and looked from father to sister. Habiba was tearing at her hair and rolling on the sandy *zaure* floor. Ummi did not know if she was to go to her sister or address the downcast figure of her father for some explanation to the reason for Habiba's strange behaviours. At that moment, Habiba stood up and walked out of the *zaure* and Ummi closely followed behind, holding on to her hand and asking questions, which the girl could not answer. Sadia saw the girls walking towards their room and she looked towards the *zaure* and saw the tip of Saleh's caftan. Habiba was still crying when she got into the room and collapsed on the floor and continued to cry. Ummi could not get any word out of her and she too began to cry. She got along with Talatu and her male siblings but it was Habiba she had always seen as her only real sister. In that same sense, anything that made her sister unhappy meant her own unhappiness. The noises that the boys and their friends made reached them from the compound. Ummi kept asking her sister questions without getting any word from her.

That night, Sadia cooked the family meal with the help of her daughter, Talatu. Ummi remained in the room with her sister and would not let her out of her sight. She was only 12 years old and yet, knew that their father had said something hurtful to make the good-natured Habiba cry so hard. Both girls refused to eat that night, in fact, Habiba was thinking about running to Kande's house because she did not imagine how she could ever face her father again.

Saleh was also heartbroken after the encounter with Habiba. He simply told Sadia that he had informed the girl whose subsequent reaction she knew. He too could not eat that night. A sudden hush fell on the house. It was as if another member had died and had to be mourned. Even the boys spoke in whispers and ate very little that night. They were sensitive to the tensed air in the house. Habiba sat in a corner in their room while Ummi lay on the mat, looking at the ceiling and thinking about the situation she and her sister faced. If their father suddenly did not want them to live with him, they could go back to their mother. She had never really hated it at her mother's house. She knew that Habiba and their mother had some misunderstanding now and again but she was their mother and she thought of seeing her again.

"If we are not happy here, can't we go back to our mother at Dalori?" she asked without turning to look towards the direction where her sister sat. For all she knew, Habiba had been happy at their father's and so was she. In her twelve years, she had lived at different homes already. The first four years were with both parents; then they moved to live with Kakalolo, their maternal grandmother, for another four years and then Sabiu's house until she was eleven and only one year at their father's and now, they did not seem to know what was to become of them.

"What are we going to do, Habiba?"

It was late in the night, the boys were sleeping in their room and Talatu was outside with her mother or at some other place within the compound. Ummi wondered why the girl was not sent in to sleep. Was Sadia afraid of them that she would not allow her daughter to come into the room with them? She continued in that way until she fell asleep. When the room was quiet, Habiba began to sob silently wishing she could die or even wake up from the terrible dream that was consuming her serene life. The night grew quiet and the cries of crickets from crevices in the cracked walls of the house swamped her brain. The silent night was still and frigid and from the distance, the howling of dogs drifted to her like the croaking of frogs from the stagnant gutters on the street that had been thumbing through her head since early evening. She had always thought the croaking of frogs was a fascinating mystery that told stories beyond man's understanding. Right then, she was in no mood for the unraveling of animal sensibilities or mysteries. She felt sore from prolonged sitting and hunger. Her eyes fell on the sleeping Ummi, lying face up on the mat and she felt sorry that she had put her sister through so much suffering. Her mind went back to her discussion with her father earlier that day. She wondered at how he could betray her in that manner. Schooling was her passion and she was determined to keep herself in school even if that meant going back to her mother, Kande. As she looked at the sleeping girl, she made up her mind that they had to move again, back to their mother's place. She hoped that one year of not living with her mother could remedy their sour relationship. She began to think of ways to get out of the house with her sister. The household, especially their father and Sadia, would be on the lookout for their possible escape. She may have to wait for the right signs, which will be when their father was out of the house. She did not think that Sadia would attempt to stop them from leaving. When she was sure of what to do in the next coming days, she stretched out her weary body, rested her head on the curves of her left hand and slept.

In the morning, Habiba woke to the clamouring of kitchen utensils. She looked to where Ummi had lain, the place was empty, Ummi was not in the room. She was surprised that she slept through the early morning call for prayers and it seemed as if the problem hovering over her had faded away. She was sure that her mother was going to object to her father's decision to have her married off so early. Cautiously, she walked to the window and watched as Ummi and Talatu sat on stools, peeling sweet potatoes. Sadia was in the sooty kitchen, perhaps, frying. That was Habiba's role, to fry because the younger girls could not be trusted with hot oil. She often wondered how it was that she began doing all the chores considered adult work at a very early age. Her mind wondered at what her father could be doing and if, in fact, he was going to go ahead with his decision to get her married. Who was she to be marrying? She did not even know the person. She watched as the smoke from the kitchen spiralled through the tiny outlets on the wall and then dissolved into the larger open air. Her Integrated Science class came to her mind immediately. She recognized the theory of dispersion, from higher concentration to lower or the other way round. She loved learning and did not want anyone to rob her of it. The boys were jumping about from the old woman's verandah to the lower ground without minding the activities in the compound. They were waiting to be asked in when the food was ready. How lucky they were, she mused. She watched as the gentle breeze made the far off Neem tree to sway and ruffle its leaves in slow motions which was exciting to the butterflies fluttering in the cool morning breeze. The wind had probably smelt sweet to them and they were out, flapping their white wings and fluttering around the leaves hoping that the slow wind would stop. She had never known that butterflies lived on trees and not hidden in thick grasses on the fields. She was even more surprised to see their cluster on that Neem tree in her father's house. She knew that they were common during the rainy season but it was not rainy season. In addition, she did not realize that they lived on big bitter trees. She shook her head and stopped to wonder what might be happening to her. Her attention moved to her sisters, busy peeling more and more potatoes and envy suddenly overwhelmed her. She envied their ages and cursed her star for growing up so fast and assuming a woman's features even when she was still a child. Hot tears rolled down her cheeks and when she was about to break into a loud sob, she covered her mouth with her left hand and ran back to the corner where she had sat the previous day. She wept hard until she felt the pains run through her heart. In her sorrow, she thought of Sadia and wondered sadly why the woman who was acting mother to her and Ummi could not say a word to her about what was going on. Was she behind all that was happening? Could she not say some words of comfort to her or dissuade her father from carrying out his plans? Why was she all eyes as though she did not belong to the family? She wondered at the possibility of the fate falling on Sadia's own daughter, Talatu, would she have then said something to stop her husband from ruining her daughter's future? The answers to all or some of those questions lay bare before Habiba. Sadia had to have known of the plan because it did not seem possible that her father did not consult her before talking to her in the *zaure*.

The sounds made by the household flooded her senses again

and she felt she was already missing her part in it. From the distant horizon, she could hear a faint rumbling that made the floor vibrate. It was a common occurrence for the tires of some big trucks to suddenly explode. She wiped her tears and sat huddled in the corner of the room waiting for Ummi to come in. It was obvious that they could not make their exit just then because everyone was busy at one thing or the other. She wondered again, what her father might be doing or where he was.

When Ummi came in with a plate of fried potatoes and two plastic cups of black tea, Habiba knew she was hungry and could not allow herself suffer the pangs of hunger since she was prepared to fight her father on his decision. As they ate, she told the younger girl that they had to go back to their mother that night. It was meant to be a secret and Ummi understood. She had so much faith in her sister and believed that she could never mean to bring her to any pains. The girl accepted whatever it was that she was told as her own way of proving to Habiba that she loved and trusted her.

The Marriage

That night, Habiba and Ummi could not escape from the house as Saleh had suspected their every move from the moment he had mentioned the matter to her. He had told the boys to watch their every movement. After supper that day, Ummi had sneaked to the dark corner in the *zaure* where she waited for Habiba to take the ablution kettle and pretend to be going to the toilet. Saleh was in his room and from there, watched the entrance. He had seen Ummi busy herself with packing onto the verandah the mat on which he had sat and other scattered items in the compound. She was not his object of interest so he paid little attention to her. Baba Audu actually saw Habiba as she made for the *zaure* and called his father.

"Baba," was all he needed to say and in a flash, Saleh was right in front of the frozen girls. As he shooed them back into the house, even he had some tears in his eyes and yet, he could not help himself. The wailing from the girls was so loud that neighbours like Mal. Hashimu and another called Kabiru, rightly thought that something major had happened and rushed in to find out. Saleh turned to them, apologized, and blamed it on children squabble.

Sadia stood on the verandah, her children within her immediate reach and said nothing. Habiba felt the betrayal in her heart as she and her sister wept bitterly. When he bade goodnight to the two men, he locked the door and walked past the girls to his room without another word. Habiba could not sleep that night. Ummi was able to sleep after a prolonged weeping in support of her sister without still having the slightest clue as to why they were experiencing all the commotions.

The following day was a Thursday. In the early hours of that day, Saleh went to see Mal. Zubairu in his house.

"Get a few of your people ready, the ceremony is better held on Saturday, 10.00 am," he said mirthlessly after they had exchanged a depressive greeting.

"Why the hurry?" he managed to ask as he displayed his fake surprise. In his heart, he knew he could never wish for anything less spontaneous, however, he had intended to show off a little wealth to the invited guests that, indeed, he had the means to keep more wives than the four permissible. He looked at Saleh from the corners of his eyes and wondered what could have prompted the hurry. Saleh was already moving away when Zubairu shouted after him, "What about the customary feast expected after the wedding?" He needed to know if he could help with that aspect since he knew that Saleh was in no position to handle anything close to hosting anyone.

"There will be no feasting."

Zubairu watched the silhouette figure of Saleh disappear at the bend as the early morning rays enveloped his shadowed contour. In his room, he sat on the bed and wondered at the man's attitude and the possible reason for the rush. Whatever it was, he intended to comply, after all, it was a two-day affair after which he would be one wife better off and ready for a new experience. He began to make his list of friends to grace the occasion barely 48 hours away. He rushed to the section he was preparing for the girl to see if Bashir, the mason, had completed the last bit of wiring in the rooms. The keys were hanging on the door when he stood by it. The fresh smell of paint tinged the air as he reached for the windows to release the latch to let in the cold air. He walked cautiously on the dusty floor to the inner room. It was smaller than the outer and it had a small window at the rear end which faced his second wife, Hauwau's section. A crooked smile flashed on his face as his thoughts went to the first night with his beautiful gazelle, Hauwau, in that inner chamber that had become his nest. He was convinced that he would always have his secret longings for her even when he was with his other wives. The problem was that she could not withstand his strength and since a man is made for more than one woman, he had to find other comforts. He inspected the toilet as well and was satisfied with Bashir's work. All that remained was to get someone to sweep and quickly clean off the paint stains on the windowpanes. He turned the keys again and walked towards his bedroom. At the far end of her section, Rabi saw him and shook her head knowingly. She wondered whose daughter it was that was going to join them again. She and her senior wife, Ramatu, had thought that the inclusion of Hauwau into the household would pacify the monstrous appetite of their husband. They knew they were wrong when Bashir began to construct the new section that stood as a constant reproach to them all. Even Rabi was in on the deal for self-pity as they watched the section progressively come to completion each day. In the face of the hushed rivalry that went on in the household, Hauwau had been the outcast. Moreover, although she was not happy about the incoming mate who would definitely usurp her position of prided wife, she looked forward to her arrival and was determined to make the newcomer her *friend*. It was going to be a paired affair henceforward. Ramatu and Rabi on the one hand, she and the incoming on the other. It was worth looking forward to.

Zubairu sat on his prayer mat and pondered at the people he was to invite to his discreet wedding. It could not be an all-comers affair because he did not know what atmosphere to expect at Saleh's house come Saturday. He knew he did not want Waziri to be there, the man was too intelligent and would suspect something went amiss that necessitated the rush. He decided on Bello and he thought of his accountant, Khalid Kumar, as a possible witness. His mind could not readily fix a third man to accompany him to the wedding *Fathiha*. He reached for a dark blue caftan he had placed on the edge of the bed when Rabi had made his bed earlier that morning. He wore the caftan, donned a *zanna* cap on his head and went to his Mercedes car. He needed to go out to the shop, see Bello about the wedding, and order some kola nuts and importantly, the boxes of clothing materials for presentation on the wedding day had to be taken care of. As he drove towards the Gamboru market, his mind went back to his meeting with Saleh earlier. He had always thought the man to be queer and the turn of event had proven that. What he had to do was complete the procedures and take what was his and let the man be; since he needed peace, he was going to give him peace. The traffic was dense at that time of the day as the heads of school children stuck out from the back seats of cars as they were being rushed to school. Those without cars to drop their children in used hired motorbikes; it was common to see seven children, four behind, and three in front of the rider struggling between cars in the early morning rush in Maiduguri. He watched the trucks ahead of him as they emitted white smoke. He was glad he had turned on the air-conditioner even though the weather was still cold. He could not tolerate the suffocating smells that came out of the rears of the firewood trucks or the sand tippers that were always out early to make quick business. It was a little past the hour of 8 am when he finally pulled off at the shop. He met the boy, Jibrin, dusting the bales of materials on the shelves. As the boy rushed out to greet him, he gave his orders directly afterwards and swung the car around and was soon on the road again.

He was going to see his head *Kususu*, the leader of the delegation that took the boxes of *toshi* to Saleh's house the previous year to ask for the hand of the girl, Habiba, in marriage. Her duties were at hand again. Aunty Yagana was the senior wife to his friend, Alhaji Bukar Alkali. That was an opportunity to tell Alhaji Bukar that the awaited marriage was at hand and he was, of course, to be one of the witnesses. He drove to his friend's compound and saw a boy washing the range of cars that graced the large compound. Alhaji Bukar was an educated man with a Higher Diploma Certificate in Commerce. He was a manufacturer of polythene bags, used by all traders for putting sold wares for customers. A very lucrative business had made him very comfortable. Zubairu had always envied his friend because to him, Bukar did business differently from him. He kept his own account books and did not need to employ an accountant as he did.

He parked his car away from the splashing water from the houseboy's hose and came out. The boy ran to him and bowed in greeting. He knew Zubairu to be his master's friend so he ran directly to inform him of Zubairu's arrival without having to stop the visitor from proceeding into the living room.

Zubairu sat on the seat directly facing Alhaji Bukar's bedroom door. It was his usual position and he did not know why he did that. Sometimes, he was early enough to catch one of his two wives, the reigning one, leaving the bedroom and he would smile slyly and remember his own *Queen of the Night* back home. Hauwau was the one that always came to his mind at times like that. It was a man's world after all and they all needed to have their fill here since the hereafter was a matter that weighed heavily on one's faith. He studied the large room and its sprawling array of custom-made cushion chairs covering the entire walls of the living room except for the three door spaces, the main entrance, and the door leading to the bedroom and the other that led to the inner part of the big house. Everywhere was a sitting place. He recognized a new picture of his friend in the midst of some youths hanging on the wall. In his hands was a large trophy which he was presenting to one of the youths in white jersey while the others stood and watched. Zubairu was not surprised to see yet another of such pictures of his friend and he wondered at how he could distribute his hard-earned resources to some clubs of whatever kind. He concluded that it was so perhaps because his friend was educated and he was not.

The boy came out of the bedroom door and informed him that the master was on his way. The morning cold air was still blowing through the main door which had no blinds. The noises of the children of the household, mixed with those of domestic birds reached him in several pitches. The imitative voice of a parrot brought a smile to his face. The bird was busy repeating a phrase that he could not make sense of but obviously, made those at hand cackle with laughter. He wondered how it was that a mere bird could speak the language of man and indeed, imitate human voices. Allah was indeed great.

The door opened and a tall man of about 53 years stepped into the room. He was the exact opposite of his friend Zubairu. Alhaji Bukar could pass for a handsome man with a glossy dark complexion and a neatly arranged set of teeth that graced his oblong Fulani-like face. He was a Kanuri man from Kukawa, Local Government Area. Zubairu shook the strong hand extended to him. His host, though many years his junior, had an air that commanded respect. Whenever he was in the presence of the man, Zubairu had always wondered what it was that made the man so confident. He was loved by most and could get whatever he set himself to because even the governor of the state, Baba Kachalla, would call him now and again for advice on matters relating not just to commerce but also on other state matters. Secretly, Zubairu knew it had to do with the fact that he was educated. There was no othe reason. In his admiration and, oftentimes, envy for this man, Zubairu had deliberately forced this friendship on the man and his family. He had made sure that he went to him for advice on matters of personal family rows in his home. Why would he not confide in the man when even the state did so?

"You are welcome. I hope that your family members are all well?"

"Everyone is well, Alhamdullilah."

"I know that business is good. I can tell that from the looks on your face," Alhaji Bukar teased.

Zubairu stretched himself on the cushion seat and a sly smiled escaped his lips. "You educated people have taken over the whole market." He was always complaining about the fact that people of his generation felt threatened by the fact that the younger business persons did better than they could because they could read and write.

"I disagree with that, Alhaji Zubairu. Who could beat you in the textile business in Borno?"

Zubairu laughed aloud filling his lungs with the gust of fresh air that blew from the open door.

"Thank you, my dear friend. I have actually come to you for yet another favour. My wedding is coming up after tomorrow."

"Why did you not say so since?" Alhaji Bukar shouted with excitement. He moved closer to his friend and whispered. "To the sweet sixteen I suppose?"

"Who else?" Both men laughed aloud, raising and stamping their feet on the carpeted floor rhythmically.

"What is the plan?"

"You of course will accompany me to the *fathyha*. It is your wife's role that is very important in all of these."

"Oh! Your Kususu?" he said pointing his forefinger at Zubairu in a mischievous way and grinning from ear to ear.

"Yes, I need her to get together her team of women to carry the wedding boxes to the home of the bride. Aunty Yagana is my ally to the end you know." He was about to add some more praises but the laughter of his friend made him stop. "What is making you laugh so?" he asked his friend who could not immediately respond. After a second look at Alhaji Bukar, he caught the bug and he too laughed.

"The devil you are. Who will it be?"

"Well, when the time comes I will see how you and your ally will continue allying," he said between laughs and wiped his face with the open side of his big *babban riga*. Zubairu looked at his friend curiously and then asked, "Do I know her?"

"You will, when the time comes." Alhaji Bukar's amusement was more from the fact that his friend did not know that he was actually eyeing his daughter, Nana. The irony that Yagana was the *Kususu* for his future father-in-law was all too intriguing. He breathed deeply and wiped his face with the ends of his large gown, smiled, firstly, because life was sweet, and it was meant to be enjoyed. What was wrong if he, too, like his friend, found a young sweet sixteen? Did it matter from whose house the pleasure came?

"I thought you said two were enough?"

"I seriously thought so but when a gem catches my fancy, I get it. Just like you." Zubairu grinned and shook his head at the same time.

"Okay, I wait. Let's finish this urgent one and then we will swing into action for the other." His friend agreed with him and when Zubairu left, Alhaji Bukar called his wife into his room and told her about the role she was going to play in the marriage.

"Mal. Zubairu will bring the boxes tomorrow evening and you know the rest."

"I will inform some of the women this evening." She wanted to complain about something but he was not interested and when he stood up to leave the living room, she knew better than call him back. As she watched him walk away, she felt angry that she had to do something to please an old man like Zubairu against the little girl, Habiba.

At about 2.00 pm on Saturday, four hours after the marriage between Alhaji Zubairu and Habiba was contracted, Saleh's house did not wear any festive mood. There were only two women to receive Aunty Yagana's team with the boxes. Four women in all accompanied the boxes to the bride's house. They placed the three boxes on an old mat next to the one on which Sadia and

Hajara, her neighbour, sat. The women sat on an equally old carpet, placed at a little distance from the two. It was as if they were visiting a bereaved family. The atmosphere was stiff and tense.

Yagana began the conversation because she needed to complete the arduous task and lead her friends out of the house. The women, except for Aunty Yagana, sat with their heads downcast. Aunty Yagana greeted the two women by condoling with them on the death of the old woman; after which she began opening the boxes for the two to see.

"Thank you, Sister. There is really no need to open any of the boxes because as you can see, we are just two and for the fact that an urgent tag has been placed on this reception, we think that we should do it speedily. Like us, we can see that you are also under some constraints." Hajara spoke the words while Sadia could only stare blankly above the heads before her.

Aunty Yagana looked at her entourage and nodded slightly in understanding. Neither side wanted to do the task, it was a burden to do. Simultaneously, they saw the role they were made to play as lacking merit but no one was in the position to ask questions as to why they had to perform them if they did not feel obliged to do so. The woman that sat next to Aunty Yagana reached out and began to zip up the open box while the others pinched one another indicating their readiness to depart.

As they took hurried steps to the waiting car outside the house, each woman was occupied with her own thoughts. Each knew it had to be a case of forced marriage. They were sorry for the girl because they knew also that she could not be saved from the brutal fate.

When the women were out of sight, Sadia looked at Hajara and shook her head.

"I cannot believe that Habiba is going to be bundled to Zubairu's house tonight."

"Poor thing." They remained seated on the mat and except for the few instances of hissing and the clicking of tongue, they said nothing. It was a vicious world for women thought Hajara and wondered why her own husband, Hashimu could not stop Saleh from selling out his daughter to the rich old man. She had never met the man, Zubairu, but from what she heard, he was a friend to Saleh's own father and that was enough to earn him her hatred.

Sadia's thought went beyond the immediate problem of her husband giving out his eldest daughter without her consent. It appeared that Saleh did not think about the household things with which a young girl is often dispatched to a husband's house. Things like her cooking wares, beddings, plates and the sort. Suddenly, they heard a loud sound from the distant fringe. The sound was becoming a routine.

In the room, Habiba also heard the sound and wished that the world could come to its end. Her mind went to a burst tire and again, she imagined that the sound was too loud for a tire explosion. Later that night, when Zubairu's emissaries came in two cars to convey the bride to her husband's house, news filtered that the frequent blasting sounds were bomb explosions from the enclave of a religious sect. For that reason, they needed to take the bride and depart as quickly as they could.

Sadia and Hajara did what they could to pacify the girl and dress her up for the departure. Ummi would not stay behind as she cried with Habiba and the women thought it better to allow them go together. Except for the clothes in Zubairu's boxes, the two girls left their father's house with nothing. Sadia and Hajara could not help themselves as they too wept out of pity for the innocent Habiba.

They were ushered into the new section meant for her when they arrived Zubairu's house. It was devoid of any form of furnishing because Zubairu expected that her own household things would accompany the girl. However, given the situation they faced and the urgency attached to it, he could understand that Saleh could not send the girl with anything to start life.

Habiba and Ummi cuddled on the carpeted floor close to each other and continued to cry. The room smelt of fresh paint. The walls were a light blue shade, a single electric fan hung in the middle of the white ceiling and the light came from a bulb that hung on the wall, almost at the entrance to the inner room. The floral curtain material had a strip of sea blue petal designs with patches of black dots around the edges. They simply sat there, not knowing what to expect from a day that had brought them so much pains. At that time, Ummi had understood what had happened to Habiba and the pains were hers just as well. She could not understand why their father had to marry off her sister in the way that he did. Like Habiba, she did not know the husband and as she wiped her tears, her eyes fell on the three boxes that accompanied them to their new abode. Three black boxes that contained the immediate clothing needs of her sister. The fact that she did not have any clothes did not bother her as long as she was with her sister. She wanted to suggest to Habiba that they could attempt the escape right then but thought otherwise. Instead, she turned to her sister and asked, "Habiba, can we send a message to our mother?"

"I was also thinking of a way to send words to her or even, to escape from this place."

Ummi was glad that Habiba was thinking of a way out. They were both sure that Kande would not allow the huge joke to continue for long, for that was what it was, a huge joke. As they talked in low tones, they heard some soft female voices discussing from the back of the room in which they sat. Ummi was first to discern the female voices because Habiba's ears were temporarily hard of hearing, perhaps from prolonged weeping. She felt some kind of heaviness in her head and it seemed like an insect had lodged itself in her brain. Ummi craned her neck and turned her right ear towards the direction of the sound. She wanted to know in whose house they were. To get answers, she needed to listen to the conversation of the women behind the room. She looked at Habiba's tear-stained face, it was drawn to its limits. What could she be thinking? she wondered and settled to occupy herself with the voices filtering through the open windows. The voices repeated the word "Alhaji" repeatedly, which did not make any sense to her since every rich man was called an Alhaji.

The night grew quiet and she was tired and sleepy, having wasted her time as it were without obtaining much information from the whispering voices. She yawned aloud and as she was putting down her cupped hands from her mouth, Habiba caught the bug and yawned too. They were both tired but sleeping in that strange environment was unbearably out of the question.

The next morning was a Sunday; the day was slow in coming. Sadia could not match the reluctance of the sun to rise from its bottomless abyss on that particular day with any she had seen in her entire life. She imagined though, that her state of mind was capable of recording the slowness of time in the book of memories, imprinted in her heart. The time it took the sun to come out was definitely slow. Saleh had not slept in the house and that to her was enough reason for time to stop. It was different from the experience of that night when the old woman had made him so angry that he had slept in the shop. She should have seen it coming. Zubairu and the old woman had a heinous alliance which had matured and had sent her husband away from his home and responsibilities.

She with her three children sat on the verandah waiting for his arrival. At the first signs of dawn, her heart began to beat a different tune from that of hope to despair. She was afraid of what could happen to them should Saleh decide to do something rash. He was a man with an enormous sense of shame and the turn of events that compelled him to sell, as it were, his first-born child to the devil would haunt him for the remainder of his life. Her eyes were dry and twitchy from prolonged weeping. She stared at the *zaure* door expectantly as if Saleh's ruffled figure would appear at any point. As she sat there, lost in thought, she heard a dull thump from the far distance. She remembered that Alhaji Zubairu's emissaries had mentioned that the sounds were bomb blasts, a new wave in the town. Her mind wondered at why people would want to blast bombs around habitations. In her mind, she knew that the economic hardship that her family and many more like them faced were the fault of the democratic government. They were busy hacking away resources belonging to the people for the comfort of their own families. From what she often heard on the radio, the stolen monies were so large that she could not fathom or understand how they could spend it.

She wiped away the gathering tears from the corners of her eyes and looked towards her children. Talatu may have noticed the shine at the corners of her mother's eyes but turned to look at her brothers whispering to one another over some unfinished game of *langa* (a one-legged race) they had begun with their friends from the neighbourhood the previous day.

Sadia was considering going out to the shop to look for Saleh but thought of getting something for the children to eat first.

Talatu was there to help her in the sooty kitchen. She could not help missing the girls and at that time, she wondered at what could have happened to Habiba at the hands of that monster, Zubairu. She had never liked the man but at the same time, she knew it was the only way out of the circumstance they all faced. Before long, she was out on the street, walking towards Saleh's shop. Her head *jallabiya* was sweeping the dusty road, picking little splinters of wood and cellophane in its wake. She greeted a man that stood beside a crowd of *Almajirai* boys (street urchins) squatting around the woman frying *kosai*. She asked, as though she wanted to purchase some commodities. He turned around to look at the kiosk before telling her that he did not believe that the shop had opened that morning.

"He married out his daughter yesterday. He may not open today." The information came from the woman frying *kosai*. Sadia felt her heart sink into the pit of her belly. Her eyes glittered from a string of tears forming in the dark interiors of her head. News could not really be hid. She was surprised at how this ordinary woman could have known the nascent secrets of her family at such short time. It was especially worrisome when the news of the marriage was thought of as a closely kept secret because of the shame of it. She thanked them, turned her back, and walked away, not towards her home but towards the motor park at the far end of the street. She boarded a bus that was loading and sat on one of the back seats. Soon other passengers were hurrying into the steaming vehicle and before she knew it, the bus was speeding along the undulating road at top speed and at the same time, the driver kept his left hand constantly on the horn, hooting as if all the people on the street were hard of hearing. Sadia wiped the large tear that fell on her cheek and looked through the window at the distant fringes. She had no destination in mind and the two hundred naira notes she had clutched in a fist felt wet. She smelt the sweat from the bodies cramped against her from both sides. She could not protect her nose from the offensive assaults of assorted odour and body cramps. In her mind again, she knew everything boiled down to the level of poverty to which the people had been reduced. At that point, her mind wondered at where Saleh could have gone. As she looked through the bus window, she searched the faces of all the men walking sluggishly on their way to fetch something to feed the teeming mouths of children they were responsible for at home. The bus stopped intermittently at designated stops and each time, people would get out and others would pigeon themselves into the little available spaces. At the end of the road, she got out of the bus and realized that she was at Mairi Village. It was called a village because in some years past, the settlement was far removed from the main town of Maiduguri. However, the influx of people into the town had swallowed all new settlements around the metropolis into a large city of people from varied backgrounds. The morning air was still cold. The wind still blew the dry harmattan breeze through her *jallabiyya*. She was not habitually a person good at looking at the faces of people when she walked but on that day, her eyes were fixed on every face that she passed. In her heart, she wondered if in fact, she could recognize Saleh if she saw him in a different setting from the one she knew. She was used to him coming back after the *Isha* prayers every evening and leaving the house at sunrise. It was, therefore, the shadowed contours of him in those moments that she was sure to identify. She walked on, wondering at herself why she headed towards Mairi in particular. She knew that Kaana lived there but she was not sure she could locate his house since she had always gone in the company of Saleh. She remembered the house had a colour that was between white and cream. The landmark she was sure of was that of a laundryman who had pitched his kiosk on the right hand side of Kaana's house. As she neared the first row of houses, there was no kiosk within view. She walked to a smaller lane that linked the bigger streets and still could not be sure to locate the house. She made a few more unsuccessful links until finally, she decided to ask a man who sat on a bench in front of his house enjoying warmth from the early sunrise. She had missed the street from the point the bus dropped her. She had to walk two streets backwards and even then, she asked for help from some youths squatted round a dying fire. After incomprehensive descriptions from several of them, the older person asked a little boy sitting at the tail of the group to take her to the house. When Kaana's house appeared before her, she felt relieved as though she had identified Saleh standing before her very eyes in the midst of the other men. She thanked the boy whose eyes fell on her fisted left hand. She knew he wanted more than her verbal gratitude but she could not help him in that respect for she had children back home, whose fate were grimmer than his. As she walked towards the door, she wondered how it was that the younger generation expected something in return for little help rendered. She wanted very much to think about the absurdity of a child expecting a reward after every errand but she had reached Kaana's house.

She pushed the door and announced her presence from the second entrance. Kaana's voice answered from within. She met him on a mat having breakfast with his sons. Bintu his wife came out on hearing a female voice. She was glad to see Sadia and asked after the children and the wedding of the previous day, which she could not attend. Sadia agreed that it was an emergency wedding and sat on the mat that Bintu placed for her on the verandah, away from Kaana's. After one or two more scoops of the gruel, Kaana left the breakfast dish wiping his mouth with the sleeves of his old *babban riga*. He sat back, leaning against the wall and exchanged a more formal greeting with Sadia. Without being told, he knew something was terribly wrong.

"What brings you so early, and where is Saleh?"

"He did not sleep at home last night," her voice was shaky as the tears welled in her eyes. Bintu was touched and exclaimed in fear, praying that he was safe. Kaana did not have a clue where to begin the search for his friend. He ran his fingers in circles scratching the itch from his budding grey hair above his earlobes and at the nape of his neck all at the same time. He scratched like someone with nits and lice in his hair and clothes. He assured her that he would find her husband and even told her that he probably was already back home. Sadia found her excitement mounting at the mention of the possibility. She could only wish at that point, to be home at once to be with her family and would not accept the breakfast tray Bintu placed before her. Kaana saw her board a bus heading to Pompomari with the promise to call on them later that day.

Habiba shrieked at the sound of the male voice in the room. She did not hear the door open and was ashamed to admit that sleep had stolen her senses. She felt like someone caught stealing because she did not think that someone in protest had the luxury of sleep, especially in the home of the tormentor. Ummi's face was drawn and the prints of the carpet were on her soft, baby face. Zubairu looked at the girls and smiled slyly. He noticed from their disposition that they had not moved from where they had sat the previous night. The boxes were still in the parlour and he packed them all to the inner room and directed them to go in and have their wash. In his heart, he knew they were just children and in a corner of that same heart, he acknowledged that the girl may have a developed womanly form but she was still a child and he needed to give her some time to settle into her new responsibility as his wife. He did not want his other wives knowing that he had not been with his new bride. As it was customary, the new bride had a weeklong honeymoon to cook for and please her groom before the routine shift continued from where it had stopped.

Habiba's heart began to race as her mind searched for a name for the man standing before them. She could not look him in the face because of his elderly nature. That was the custom. She knew she had heard the voice and seen the figure before but where and when she could not immediately recollect. When they were alone again, they asked one another where they had seen the man, who was obviously the husband in whose house she was. Habiba felt the bile come to her throat and her face was immediately bathed in tears. She wondered how her own father could do a thing like that to her. At that moment, she was sure she could stab him with a knife and stab herself if only to prove the gravity of the betrayal to the world. The pain of it ran through her blood settling finally in the cage of her young heart. It was so tangible, so solidified she could locate it with the tip of a pin, it laid concealed within her own body, causing her such grave pain. She wished her heart to fail but life did not always just come and go by merely wishing it to. Ummi too had tears in her eyes, although she could never feel the heaviness of Habiba's soul. It was the sort of burden which no one but the owner could carry.

The sun shining through the drawn curtains fell on the wall behind them. Habiba imagined that Sadia and her children were, perhaps, eating breakfast and her father smiling and selling in his shop, pretending that all was well while they were horded out of the way. Was the arrangement convenient for Sadia and her father? Did her mother, Kande know of the arrangement? In her heart, she knew that Kande did not know of the fate that had befallen her. Not that they had any form of harmony in their relationship, she wished all the same that her mother would be told of what she was facing if she did not already know. Even for the sake of Ummi who had pitched her fate to hers, she wished her mother to know.

The door opened and a girl, about Ummi's age, walked in with a large tray on which three dishes were carefully set. There was a shocked expression on her face as she set the tray before them. Her greetings were hardly audible. As she turned to leave the room, Habiba called after her and thanked her for the food.

"What is your name?" she spoke in Hausa to the girl whose face was suddenly alive with excitement. Like the girl, Ummi was also transposed from her thoughts and, indeed, fears.

The girl walked closer to where Habiba sat and said softly, "My name is Rakiya." Her bare feet made some scuffing movement on the carpet.

"Thank you, Rakiya. What is your father's name? The owner of the house, is he your father?" Habiba did not want to expose herself more than it was necessary.

"He is my father."

"What is his name?" Ummi seeing the confusion her sister was in, chipped in. They waited as the girl looked from one to the other before answering.

"Alhaji Zubairu. You mean you do not know him?"

"Of course, we know him. He left this very room a short while ago." Ummi looked at her sister whose expression went gob-smacked. The muscles on her face were visibly working up and down in a futile effort to communicate at least, with her sister. Sensing trouble, she quickly sent the girl away, a forced smile playing on her face. Habiba felt limp and lethargic like a drowning person weighed down by a huge stone. As soon as they were alone, Habiba began crying again. Ummi's eyes fell on the tray of food but she could not touch it. Her stomach rumbled from hunger made worse by the sight of the tray. She was sure the food would taste nice for a pleasant aroma wafted into her nostrils. She could not remember the last time they had their last normal meal. "Alhaji Zubairu?" she heard her sister say in a whisper and immediately, her hunger was secondary.

"That must be the man we greeted that night Kaka was sitting in front of her room?"

Habiba only nodded in reply and wiped the tears from her face.

"Ummi, you have to go to our mother and tell her what has happened."

The younger girl looked at her sister wide-eyed, not knowing what to say. She was wondering how she was going to locate her mother's house all by herself since Habiba had always been her lead. At that moment, the reality of her own existence began to dawn on her. She was no longer going to have the comfort of having her older sister watch over her every action. With the back of her left hand, she wiped away a large tear that came down her face.

"I may not know my way to Mother's house, Habiba."

"I will describe the way and draw the route on a piece of paper for you.

She may be able to help me, Ummi."

The girl watched her closely and nodded. She knew that Habiba could no longer go out without her husband, Alhaji Zubairu's permission. She was to live in *purdah* like most married women in the area. Before they finally touched the food, it was afternoon. The room had become silent and Habiba had called on the crouching Ummi to eat some of the food brought in by the girl, Rakiya. The sight of food has a way of aggravating one's hunger for she began to salivate and in the end, they were rushing the food as though someone they could not see was chasing them.

Later that afternoon, men moving in a set of settees waked them from deep sleep. They arranged the furniture, placed an ebony coloured bed, mattress and linen, with a set of drawers in the inner room, and went out without saying anything to the two girls with their ambivalent faces.

Alhaji Zubairu sat on the carpeted floor in his room, a large tray with half-closed dishes, serving spoons, dirty plates and some plastic cups was set at a corner away from where he sat. He had sent for one of his young daughters to take the tray away. His mind went to the movements of men moving in and out of the large compound with the items he had ordered for the girl, Habiba. He felt a sense of regret almost at the turn of events. He had not expected that Saleh was going to put up a fight with him over the desire to marry his daughter as he did. A fight was good when the warring sides were equally matched. Here he was, fighting a drowning man and to him, that fact eroded the pleasure he had hoped to get. He felt sorry for the girl though who was not sent forth with any of the required household things. He had decided to do for her those things her father was unable to do. Especially, to get all that she needed to function normally in his home. The strange circumstances that greeted the marriage were unavoidable and he was willing to allow the girl some time to get used to her new environment before making any demands that were by right his. His thoughts went to his daughter, Nana, who was about Habiba's own age. He convinced himself that he was going to be tolerant in his dealings with the girl. He wondered how it was, that people often thought him selfish and wicked when, indeed, he knew he was not. People often thought that when you were rich, then you could forfeit all pursuance of wrongs done to you. He was a man who believed in punishing all wrongdoers so that they behaved properly at other times. A male voice at the entrance alerted him and he answered by asking the person in.

"We have arranged all the items, Alhaji."

"Good, meet Mr Kumar for your fee," he said in Hausa without turning to look at the man at the door.

"Thank you, Alhaji."

Zubairu did not respond because he was already thinking of how to initiate the breaking of the melon, perhaps that night as he could no longer wait. Had he not already waited too long for it? From when the old woman was alive, he had looked forward to it and now that he was in possession of it, he was behaving like an old, toothless dog with a large bone before it. He felt anxious and as the excitement rose from his groins reaching to his brain, he knew that he could not wrench out desire from his genes even if he was a hundred years. It was the way that Allah created men. His mind went to his encounter earlier that morning with Ramatu, his eldest wife. She had wondered why he asked her to get his breakfast when he had taken a new bride. He had no answer for her as he fell on the bed as though she was not referring to him. Ramatu knew him better than his other wives and sensing that he did not want to discuss the matter, she had left him and had called on her children, Nana and Rakiya, to begin the preparations for their father's breakfast. Over the years, she had begun to see herself more like his sibling or even his mother instead of his wife. The mother image seemed also to have suited him as it gave him the leverage to discuss with her all the problems that his younger fancies created for him. He could even place his head on her bosom and yet, that warming sensation that sent him raving like a maniac in the presence of Hauwau would be absent. He knew that the degeneration of their erotic lives was traceable to the fact that she had suddenly began to call him 'Baba', the way their children did. Why should she call him that and not expect him to feel maternal attachment to her? It had begun like a joke one day when their first child together, Jummai (now married), was young. Jummai could not pronounce the word 'Baba' and instead said 'Dada' each time and the mother, stressed out from repeating the word caught the bug herself. That was then, when Ramatu herself, was a young bride kept in another compound away from his two earlier wives Issata, mother of Liman and Mohammed; and Balira, who bore only Sanusi for him. Those were the days when he too was a young man. He looked around the room for something to occupy his mind. Finding none, he picked his *dan chiki* caftan, dropped it from his head down, and went into the compound. He was going to see the newcomer to the household; so he picked his steps to her door. From another end of the compound, he heard Hauwau's voice in conversation with someone whose voice he could not make out. His mind told him that the women were most likely talking about his new bride. Women and their gossip, he thought, but that was all they could do since they could not stop him from fulfilling his rights. At the door to Habiba's apartment, he coughed a little to announce his entrance. He stopped by the door on seeing the girls still seated in the parlour and still wearing their clothes from last night.

"Habiba, will you stand up immediately and clean yourself up? What do you think is the meaning of this?" he was vividly angry.

The girls were startled and without a word in reply, Habiba stood up and went into the inner room and Ummi who did not want to be left in the room with the angry man closely followed her. When they were out of his sight, Zubairu walked out of the room and almost ran into Hauwau who was seeing off her friend. The woman smiled a knowing smile and looked towards the opposite side while her friend was exchanging greetings with her husband. She too was wondering why it was that he had not taken his new bride to them for introduction as it was customary. He ignored her coldness and headed to his own section. He was actually blaming himself for acting immaturely by allowing a day to pass without taking what was his by right. What was he thinking? he wondered. That night, after his dinner, he sent his little son, Bala, to call Habiba to his section.

"Tell her I need to see her now and do not come without her, okay?" he spoke Hausa to his entire household.

"Okay, Baba."

The boy met Habiba and Ummi in the inner room. They had made the bed with the flowered bedspread they had found in one of the side drawers. Although it was a difficult situation for Habiba, she could not hide the fact that back home in her father's house, not even Sadia's room was half as beautiful as the one she was in. In what seemed like magic, the two girls found themselves actually loosening up. With the ease from fetching water from a tap that ran just from applying a gentle pressure on the head, they had taken their bath in a clean bathroom smelling of new paint. Ummi was prancing excitedly on the bed like a mare while Habiba felt comfortable lying on the deep green carpet covering the entire floor. The entire place smelt of fresh paint. The frame surrounding the bed emitted the smell of turpentine, which in itself, added to the sharp tint in the air that made up the room.

"Baba is calling Habiba," the boy told the girls when he walked into the room. Ummi's joy came to an abrupt end. Habiba sat up and looked at Ummi without saying a word. Her heartbeat began to race and she told herself that she was wrong to have thought of being happy even if it was for a blink moment. Immediately, her mind went to what she was going to tell the man and wondered why he was asking to see her in the first place. She gave the boy a long look and finally decided to go with him but not without her sister.

"Ummi, let us go." She was very casual in her manners and without any time wasted, they followed the boy as he led the way to his father's section. At the door, the boy announced their presence. Alhaji Zubairu was sitting on a multi-coloured Chinese carpet set at the foot of a large bed. He noticed the presence of the younger girl and a smile came upon him. Except for the light from the television, the room was dark. He dismissed his son and when they were alone, he asked the girls to sit down. With their heads bowed down, they sat by the door, away from the Chinese carpet on which he sat. He enquired if they had eaten that evening because he had ensured that food was sent to them each time. Habiba's heart was beating so fast that she feared the man would see her dress heaving up and down even in the dark room.

"I am sure, Habiba, that you know I am your husband now?" his voice was low and croaky. The girl did not say a word. She felt a cold, moist hand touch hers and she looked at Ummi's face. The little reflection of light on her face could tell her nothing about what she thought of the man's statement.

"I do not know what your father told you before you were brought here. By law, you and I are husband and wife and as it is expected, we have to be seen to be performing the roles that bind us together." Even he did not expect that the girl had a response to that, so he continued.

"You will pass the night here while your sister will return to your room and await your return." The cold hand tightened its grip on Habiba's equally sweaty hand. They felt like their worlds had come to its end. Habiba began to sob silently as she felt Ummi's hand slip out of her grip. By that time, Alhaji Zubairu was standing above them and was actually ushering Ummi out of the room. Habiba looked at her little figure in the dark night making its way through the pavement adjoining Zubairu's room.

She could tell from the bent posture that Ummi was weeping and utterly frightened of going back there alone and having to sleep all by herself in a strange environment. Zubairu looked at her, closed the door and jammed the latch in position. He went back to the carpet and sat on it. Suddenly, he felt shy and out of words to explain to the girl before him his real intention. He finally began with little talks about the accessories that were placed in her section of the compound. He rambled over the kitchen, the plates and dishes, trays, and other little nothings like matches and knives. When she said nothing in response, he crawled towards her on his knees. She looked towards him and made way for him to pass if he needed to, but he was not going to pass her. He reached out for her headscarf, pulled it off and ran his large palm over her head in a manner that suggested a desire to caress. She felt his thick fingers scratch at her scalp roughly. Her nylon headscarf fell off as his huge hand heavily weighed on her head. She made a move to dodge but his fingers were searching through the weave of her hair, tracing the hair plaiter's lines as lovers do. She could not withstand his busy hands all over her body. She attempted a struggle by which time, he had enclosed her in a tight embrace while his other hand was fondling with her left breast, closely cropped to her chest. She wanted to scream as she was taught to do since she was five years old. Kande had warned her that her breast was never to be fondled by the opposite sex, much less the little slit between her thighs. In a matter of seconds, he was over her and she was lying on her back. She opened her mouth, a stifled cry escaped and in the confusion that she found herself, she decided to scratch and bite him wherever she could. He seemed suddenly to be in a great hurry so he pressed his hardness against her soft skin. She was resolved not to give in and her purity and innocence remained intransigent in the face of her ordeal. His breathing was heavy and in between every deep breath, he bellowed such vile swear words that only aggravated her anger. His rancid smelling sweat, dripped on to her face and she felt exasperated by the frigidity around her. When he could no longer bear what he thought was her insolence, he slapped her hard on the face, she saw white light engulf the room, and that was it. In a sadistic mood, he tore through her flesh, pouring his stored up bile into her stomach. Moments later when she reopened her eyes, her lap was smeared by a slimy mollusc that was yet to dry and had an itchy sensation. She attempted to sit up but felt a weight around her waist. She could not explain what it was. Her eyes roamed the dark room. The television was turned off and the ray of light from the electric bulb outside the room was not bright enough for her to see if her tormentor was somewhere lurking in wait. She coughed and felt warm moisture oozing out of her body. She was in pain. She wondered how an old man like Alhaji Zubairu could do that to her. How was she to face her sister Ummi without explaining to her what had transpired? He was like a thief that stole from the dead; after all, she was unconscious and felt and saw nothing until he was done with her. She remembered a passage she had read from one of her school Readers of some soldiers who stole money and other necessities from dead enemies and how some of the moralists did not approve of the theft of money but would permit robbing the dead of items like torches, cigarettes and the sort. Habiba knew that stealing was stealing and could not be qualified by the nature of the item stolen. In her case, Zubairu had stolen from her when she was in a state of unconsciousness, the chastity she had cultivated since age five. Where was the man's pride? She heard a faint sound from another part of the room and knew then that he was in the bathroom. She quickly forced herself up, grabbed at her wrapper, reached for the latch on the door and walked into the cold night air outside carrying with her, his shame which he had left her to carry. The agelong shame that is as old as man. She met Ummi sprawled in sleep on the carpet in the parlour. She was thankful for that at least. She went straight to the bathroom to see the damage done to her body and to cry in solitude. She did not want Ummi to continue to suffer on her account, so she needed an easy way out for both of them. As she cleaned herself, she thought of her father and the feeling of hatred for him overwhelmed her. She swore to herself and at the same time assured herself of the burning desire to stab him the next time she set eyes on him. It was his fault she had to go through all that she faced that night. The pain between her legs radiated to her lower abdomen. She remembered the discussion with Ummi to fetch their mother to come to their rescue. She needed someone to help her get out of that house that was, paradoxically, a grandiose paradise for her miseries.

ༀ‖ Saleh ‖ༀ

After the *Fathiha* that day, Saleh did not wait to thank the few people that attended the occasion. He had simply walked away from the small crowd. Kaana had seen him go towards the shop and had wondered what it was that he was up to but could not call after him as his attention was drawn by Mallam Hashimu's talk about the new religious sect that had claimed responsibility for the new wave of bombings rocking the town. Nothing else was on the lips of every resident; people were concerned for their lives, they could not move freely as no one knew where or when the bombs were going to blast. Kaana needed to find out where Saleh had been. The marriage was in its fourth month and he was tired of lying to Sadia over the whereabouts of her husband. Quite apart from that, he did not see himself shouldering the responsibilities of both his family and that of his friend's for much longer. In fact, it was always his fear of keeping two families simultaneously that had kept him from taking a second wife. He alighted from a bus at the Pompomari layout some distance from Saleh's street. His intention was to visit some of Saleh's friends like Mallam Garba who lived at the far end of Pompomari layout. He believed they could have some clues as to where he was. He had visited Mallam Garba once, at the instance of the death of his first wife, that was some four years back. He walked the remaining distance while his thoughts kept running in circles in his head. The sun emerged from underneath the belly of clouds from the east. Early morning businesses like puff-puff, *kosai* and *kwokwo* sellers were scattered all over the place and were each attending to their numerous customers, mostly children, sent by their lazy mothers who were not able to wake early enough to prepare the morning meals for their families. He felt his stomach cry because he could not wait for Bintu to serve his share of the morning meal before going out in search of his friend. The smell from the gutters hit his nose as he walked through a narrow lane. He wondered why the gutters smelt more in the mornings. He wanted to cover his nostrils from the violent acrid attack on his person so early in the morning but thought otherwise because he did not want the few men sitting on benches in the frontage of their houses to think their environment repulsed him and, indeed, give the impression that he was better than they were. All he could do in that circumstance was hold his breath and walk, as quickly as he could manage, through the lane. He cleverly walked the lane not daring to step on any of the numerous black cellophane bags thrown outside from homes or even abandoned by the wayside by their original owners because he knew he could be stepping on human faeces strewn in bags. His head faced down all the time; he had not realized that he had walked a great distance until he heard someone call his name. He stopped suddenly, looked towards the voice, and recognized Mallam Garba sitting on a long bench with two other men. With a smile of relief on his face, he found himself jumping over a big gutter that stood between him and the men. When he approached him, his outstretched arm touched each man's cold palm in greetings, after which he filled the little space they made for him on the bench. They chatted heartily for a little while about the recurrent bombings that were going on in the town and wondered if the perpetrators were actually indigenes of Borno. They continued in their wonder of the new advancement in terrorism and the ease with which bombs were planted in crowded areas like market-places, places of worships, bars and others like them. The sun shone brightly above the Neem trees and men and women were hurrying to work or some other engagements, not giving any thoughts to the cold breeze. Schoolchildren close to the heels of their older brothers hurried off to school even as the voices of Qur'anic pupils reciting their verses from a nearby *Stangayya* (Qur'anic school) enveloped the environment. Kaana whispered to Garba and they excused themselves from the two men and stood at the entrance to Garba's own house.

"I came to ask you about Saleh. The wife came to see me and told me he had not slept at home since the day of his daughter's marriage," Kaana finished, leaving Garba to assume that there was more to it than met the eyes.

If he suspected Kaana of knowing what he did not, he did not reveal in his zonked out eyeballs. The story was very easily shocking and he too wondered how Saleh's wife was coping. He did not know the whereabouts of their friend, Saleh, but he would ask other close associates of his. Kaana left Garba a disappointed man. He was going to Sadia to advise her to return to her people if he did not show up in a few more days. He could not imagine what else he could do for his friend. When he was face to face with Sadia, however, he could not come out looking at her face fixedly to tell her to abandon her matrimonial home and return to her people without exhausting all available options. Rather, he begged her to be patient and to pray hard for his safe return. How could he say anything else when the bond of friendship between him and Saleh was so solid? After his departure, Sadia, surrounded by her children, wept bitter tears as she pondered at the options open to her. To return to her people was not an option at all because they were, simply put, just managing to survive themselves. How could she then add four more mouths to their problems? Moreover, Kaana had done his best by them, she could not therefore ask anything more of him.

The thoughts of Habiba and Ummi suddenly came to her. The girls had turned out to be luckier in the turn of events. She rearranged her sitting position and wondered if she could not, in fact, pay them a visit. The thought was brilliant and she felt relieved that it had come to her so long after the marriage of the girl, Habiba. By the custom of their people, the mother of the bride was expected to visit the home of her newly-wed daughter to see how settled she was in her new abode. That was something she could not do because Saleh had disappeared soon after the *Fathiha*. Talatu looked at her from the corner of her eyes and could not believe the sudden loosening of all the tightness from her mother's face. She observed that the creases smoothened quickly into the coffee complexion and her mother's face was again cheerful. At first, she looked towards the *zaure* to see if her mother had seen her father walk into the compound. Seeing no one, she stole glances at her mother and then consoled herself with the fact that adults were seers and children like her could never understand some of the things they did.

At a little after 2.00 pm of that same day, Sadia, accompanied by her son, Baba Audu, walked into Zubairu's large compound. She shook off the splinters of wood and other dirts that her *jalabiya* picked on the way. Her son held on to her left hand tightly and gazed at the large compound. She stood for a while, not knowing which of the flats was housing Habiba. After a while, she headed towards the flat nearest to her, which turned out to be Zubairu's own section of the house. There was no one in sight. She greeted aloud from where she stood by way of announcing her presence, looked around and still, there was no response from anyone. Baba Audu called out in his shrill, childish voice, still no one came to them. Sadia wondered if there were people in the house at all. She did not want to contemplate going back home without seeing Habiba and indeed, Alhaji Zubairu. What were she and her children to live on if she should turn back? No, she had to see someone. The sun was shining brightly and the sweat was pouring from her temple down to her neck and making its way through her armpit and breasts. She looked at her son who had found an old tin to sit on. Suddenly, a boy of about four dashed out of the farthest compound, crying. He was Ramatu's grandson, Usman. The boy ran towards them and stopped suddenly on seeing Baba Audu. He paid no attention to the woman standing in black, it was the boy a little older than he was that caught his attention and he stood there, open-mouthed with his unshed tears still filling his large eyes. He was scared, especially of the woman and he wanted to retreat backwards but Sadia called to him. He stopped, looked at the boy first, then at her. When she asked him of his mother, he ran back into the house screaming at the top of his voice. Not long after that, Nana came out of the door and Sadia met her midway.

"Please, we are looking for Habiba," she spoke in Hausa.

"There," she pouted her lips towards Habiba's section of the house.

Sadia thanked her and dragged her son towards the door to Habiba's part. When she greeted at the door, Ummi thought she was dreaming because she could recognize the voice even in her sleep. She ran to Habiba's side and whispered, "Habiba, Auntie Sadia has come." Habiba's eyes opened wide in disbelief.

"What is the wicked woman looking for now?"

"Who knows? Should she come in?" Ummi asked just as Sadia's voice was calling out for the third time. Ummi went to the door and ushered the woman and her son into the parlour where Habiba was. As they entered, Habiba stood up to welcome them. At the sight of the woman who she thought had a hand in the misfortune that had befallen her, Habiba's face immediately assumed a contortion that spelt hatred. Sadia recognized the sickening look on the girl's face but could not have imagined the magnitude of her displeasure at her presence. Ummi too noticed the change in her sister, and that quickly decided for her the mode of salutation she offered her step-mother. After the initial greetings, a solemn air enveloped the room. Habiba looked down all the time and played with her toes. Sadia suddenly realized that she could not look the girls in the face. She kept reassuring herself that it was their father who did the wrong; that is if any wrong had been done in the first place. Why did she then feel remorseful? She hated herself for feeling guilty. She wanted to ask the girls some questions but could not bring herself to it, how could she leave without finding a solution to the problem that took her there? She thought of the other children back home and tears welled in her eyes.

"Since the day of this marriage, your father has not been seen by anyone." Her eyes were downcast as she opened up to them.

Habiba looked at her and asked, "Why?"

"Allah alone knows why. That is why I came to see Alhaji."

"I see," Habiba responded disinterestedly. She looked at her sister's face and finding no readable expression, she added, "We know nothing about his movements, but you can enquire from his household."

Sadia caught the bitterness and, indeed, hatred in the girl's voice and felt sorry for their entire handicap. She knew that her visit was far from being welcomed so, she immediately stood up and holding her son's right hand, bade goodbye to them and walked towards the first flat, where she had met Nana. Her meeting with Zubairu was a lifeline for her and the children and her patience had to be elastic. She noticed with utmost dismay that neither of the girls looked towards Baba Audu, their own brother. It appeared to her also that they did not even care if their father never returned. At the entrance to Ramatu's compound, Sadia cleared her voice and greeted. Again, the girl Nana came out to attend to her. "Please, I wanted to know when Alhaji will return," she said in a voice that was only a little more than a shaky whisper.

"I cannot tell, but you can check him in the evening." Sadia thanked the girl and pulled her son towards the main gate.

After Sadia's departure, Habiba's thoughts went wild. She remembered how two days to the wedding, her father had called her outside in the *zaure* again, just like the first time, and had made her a fatherly promise to get her out of the mess he was about plunging her. How could he disappear from home when she was working in line with his plans for her, albeit, with resistance? What could have made him to disappear from home without fulfilling his promise to her? *"My child, do not shame your father in his time of need."* His words re-echoed in her brain. She had raised her face to look at his tear-stained face in the faintly diffused twilight. That night, she had wept and had rebounded with him in the love that could only exist between a father and his daughter, his firstborn child. Moreover, when he had begged her to work in accordance with his plans, how could she fault her own beloved father? *"I will get you out, you will go to school and become a Veterinarian but for now, you will have to trust me, my child. I need you to oblige him for a very short period so that he would have no reasons to demand anything from me."* It was a pact between a father and child. Where did she go wrong in all of this?

That evening, Sadia met Alhaji Zubairu sitting on his usual Turkish carpet outside the gate, having had his supper with some of his sons. He did not know who she was when she squatted before him that evening. How could he recognize her when he had never looked into her face even in the nights when he visited them back then when the old woman was alive? He was shocked to know that Saleh had not returned since the day of his marriage to Habiba. What was he to say about his bride except to hope that she would settle down in time and bear him strong sons? He reflected on the three encounters he had had with her since the marriage and a wicked smile played on his lips. He saw a good opportunity in the coming of the woman as one that could easily win his new bride over to his disposal.

"Go back home to your children, I will see what I can do tomorrow." Sadia thanked him profusely and wept for joy as she walked home.

That night, Alhaji Zubairu sent for Habiba to come into his room. It was not her turn to cook for him. She had begun to cook in the new kitchen he had fixed for her. She was shocked that he would want to see her even though it was not her turn. As she went into the inner room to pick her veil, she told Ummi that she was suspecting it had something to do with Sadia's visit. She found him sitting as usual on the small carpet by his bedside. The light from the TV was the only illumination that the room had. This was typical of him, so she sat at an adjacent spot that had become her usual spot. He smiled to himself when he saw her downcast head covered in a flowered veil.

"Your father's wife came to see me today," he said casually.

"Tau," she responded in Hausa meaning "Okay".

"Your father left home over a week ago and has not returned and no one seems to know his whereabouts."

"Tau."

"Your father's wife, does she do anything? I mean like trading?"

"No." The monosyllabic response had become her trademark and he was learning to get less offended by it. After all, she was a mere child and he had to employ his wisdom to get what was rightly his. He needed her to know the great favours that he was undertaking for her family on her behalf. With that accomplished, he dismissed her. He had intended to fondle her but thought otherwise, *be as cunning as the serpent* he told himself and bade her goodnight.

The next day, Alhaji Zubairu sent a pick-up van to Saleh's house at about 11.00 am. Two labourers offloaded two 50kg bags of rice, 100kg bag of beans, 2 tins of vegetable oil, a carton of maggi cubes seasoning, two cartons of pasta and the sum of twenty thousand naira in an envelope. Sadia and her children could not believe their eyes. They thanked the men so much that one would think they were their benefactors. Life for Sadia and her children again became normal. She went back to Alhaji

Zubairu's house that evening to thank him for his kindness.

"I am one of you now, am I not?" he had queried. She had nodded in complete agreement. How could she think otherwise? She walked cautiously out of the compound stealing a quick glance at Habiba's section.

She did not see any need to see the girls, after all, Zubairu had solved their problems. What else could she ask for? She did not particularly want to see their drawn faces poked towards her as if she was solely the one guilty of keeping Habiba in Zubairu's house.

"I am one of you now, am I not?"

"Haba, Alhaji, you are our father now and my children and I will forever be grateful for this kindness. Allah knows how to provide for his own. He took away my right hand and replaced it with two right hands. How could I have known that I am a favoured woman until now? My children and I will not beg for alms on the streets because you are there for us, I can only pray that Allah (SWT) continues to replenish all that you have given out in charity. May your family never know a fate where they will seek assistance from strangers" All the while, she was pronouncing her supplications, he kept muttering "Ameen, Ameen." He saw in the woman a hope akin to that of a dying man rescued from the jaws of a hyena. In the light of the saviour that he had become to the woman and her children, he expected that the helps that he was able to render to the many needy mouths around her would reciprocate and keep his family intact. That was his need in the arrangement. After all, much was required of him in return for a little favour he hoped to get from Habiba.

Talatu came some five weeks later to tell Habiba of her husband's kindness to them. Habiba and Ummi looked at one another when they heard what the girl had to say. Evidently, the girl had not visited them to see how they were or even to tell them of Zubairu's kindness five or six weeks ago. They could almost swear that Talatu was in the house to see Alhaji Zubairu for more supplies. Habiba's marriage to Alhaji Zubairu was then in its sixth month. Saleh had not returned from wherever it was that he went and no one had any concrete news of him. Some people said he had joined the new religious sect that was at war with government in all ramifications but there was no proof as to the truth of the matter. Others simply concluded that he had died and advised Sadia to consider accepting the many offers for marriage that were coming her way. At that instance, the responsibility of Sadia and her three children fell solely on the shoulders of Alhaji Zubairu. He was responsible for every drop of water spilled in the house, the children's school fees, clothing, health and even the rent on the house. It was at that instance that Habiba was struck by a bout of vomiting, the kind that she had never known in her almost sixteen years. She had become increasingly slow at everything, and could not hold down any food. She could not even bear cooking her husband's meals. At times like that, she was thankful that Ummi was still with her and could prepare Alhaji's meals. When it was her turn to sleep in his apartment, she could not go to him and he had to come to see for himself what it was that prevented her from playing her role as wife.

He wore a deep blue caftan that opened from under his armpit to his knees. His chubby face shone under the electric bulb giving it the appearance of a mischievous child smeared with petroleum jelly. His eyes roamed the room and the two girls in it. His interest was Habiba and when his eyes fell on her slouched body on the floor, he did not need a second opinion to know what she was suffering. That sly smile played on his face and he felt satisfied with himself. His smile was all knowing. She was his after all; he never believed that a woman had other options when she was so defeated. He could swear that the girl herself had no idea what she was suffering from. Therefore, when he left her section, he went straight to Ramatu's side because he knew that Habiba needed a mother figure to help her get through her new experience. When he had told her what he needed her to do, Ramatu shook her head pitiably at her old husband who did not realize his folly in making young girls, the ages of his grandchildren, his bedmates. She wondered when he was going to stop his excessive drive for the company of women, especially those much younger than he was. However, she reluctantly agreed to visit the girl the following morning. She had only met the melancholic girl a couple of times and already, she felt sorry that she had also fallen victim to the old fox in spite of the fact, which they heard, that she had not wanted the marriage in the first place.

Habiba's condition continued unabated and as rightly observed by Alhaji Zubairu, she did not know why she could not be her old self. Even more worried was Ummi who thought that her sister was definitely struck by a horrible disease that even Alhaji Zubairu could not help. She wanted to share in the pains that Habiba was going through but knew how impossible that was. When she prayed, she sat for longer periods on the prayer mat wishing that Allah would transfer whatever her sister suffered to her. She hated her father for abandoning them to that sort of fate and wished she could see her mother as they had earlier made plans to. It was her sole responsibility to nurse Habiba, she stood on her and handed her water, her medicines, and at other times, the sort of food she could tolerate like *kunun tsamia* (tamarin and millet gruel) and the like.

Ramatu announced her presence at the door the next morning and walked into the room. She met Habiba lying on the floor. The girl was visibly pale and dehydrated and was without any doubt, with child as the old fox himself had guessed. She called Ummi out to the kitchen and showed her how to prepare a mixture of oral rehydration for her sister. She reassured them both that it was a normal process, which called for no worries. It was only after that visit did the girls realize that Habiba was to be a mother. Neither of them could believe what had happened. Habiba wept bitterly and knew that her life had been terminated permanently by the development. Although she knew how the pregnancy came to be, Ummi had no idea that her sister and the old Zubairu had any form of understanding to the extent that she could be with his child. How was Habiba to explain to the thirteen-year-old that Zubairu had raped her each time she was asked to visit him? How was she to begin to explain that pregnancies could occur even when the body was not receptive of what the other was doing to it? Alternatively, how was she to give vent to the fact that Zubairu laid his old roughened hands on her soft youthful skin because she was a naïve, obedient child to their father? Everything had happened so fast that even she, at age sixteen, was talking and thinking like an adult. She felt like killing herself, even though she was well aware that it was a grave sin to do so. She had to find a way of hurting both Zubairu and her father.

She thought of running off into prostitution like all the young girls of her age that have rented rooms on their own behind Gwamari ward but after much consideration, she knew she could not withstand the rigours. And also, she saw herself as already performing the same task in Zubairu's house, the only difference being that he was her only client. At the same time, she did not want to accept the horrible fate of staying with a man like Zubairu while her father walked away a free man. How could she allow them the success on a platter of gold without retribution? In all that she suffered, it was her father that she blamed the most. She had loved and trusted him without reservations and had preferred him to Kande, their mother. How could she, after all that had happened, distinguish between love and hate? As far as she was concerned, one either loved absolutely or hated perfectly. Often, she had asked herself if there was the *in between* in loving and hating. Could love and hate merge to give birth to something that was not completely love or hate, something that was a little in between the two? If there were, what would that thing be called? Could she, therefore, love the thing Alhaji Zubairu had deposited in her body even though she hated him so? What and indeed, how was she to view the child when it was eventually born? Could the hate that she felt for it easily become an elixir to her fate and indeed, destiny in later life? What was the meaning of the life that they lived? Was everything about life situated between white and black, good and evil, thin and fat, love and hate, brave and coward and so forth? Are there the in betweens of our existence? She could not place her father or Alhaji Zubairu for that matter in all of these, because they seemed like floats on the surface of an ocean that were tossed by the vicissitudes of greed, cowardice and selfishness that determined their every action. Her father's treachery was by far crueler than the lethargic state that Zubairu had condemned her. In her mind's eyes, she saw herself in some years to come: a half-illiterate, old woman with numerous children because she knew there was no escaping for her, at least, not with Sadia's new moves because as it were, they had to survive. From a remote part of her heart, she knew that she needed to assume a state of mind to keep her sanity. A disposition that would invariably compel Zubairu to send her away was what she had to work on finding.

Ummi interrupted her thoughts when she handed her a cup of oral rehydration, and she had to pause to take a decision and give a name to that thing which stood a little between life and death.

Mother Nature

It was thundering and lightning in quick successions, the terrifying sounds seemed to descend from the heavens with such loud bangs that were deafening. The compound was awash with light even though electricity had been cut out and the splatter of hard substances on the aluminium roof was proof that it rained hailstones. The moon seemed not to have diminished as the sky was still bright. It was cold and everywhere was silent except for the regular sounds made by the heavy raindrops as they droned ceaselessly. Ummi stood by the window to their apartment and watched as the run-off water rushed through the small openings on the fence to find outlets to lower gradients beyond their compound. The mango tree in the compound was swinging from side to side in total defiance of the pressure to it. Other smaller fruit trees like the Indian guava and the custard apple shrubs were seriously being undermined as they were forced to nose-dive downwards. Their heavy fruits dropped on the dark sands. It was a heavy rain and as she stood, watching from the comfort of her sister's home, she knew that elsewhere, many families would be homeless or have nowhere to lay their heads for the night as roofs were very likely to have been blown off by the strong winds or leaking roofs which were a common phenomenon could undermine the sleeping places of others. As she stood by the window, lost in her own thoughts, she felt a soft hand touch her from behind and she turned to face a frightened child whom she had placed on the bed to sleep in the inner room. They were alone in the flat because the child's mother, Habiba, had gone into the larger compound to see Rabi, Alhaji Zubairu's second wife and Ummi realized that Habiba had suddenly developed the strange habit of abandoning her and her son, Abba, in her own apartment and staying long hours at Rabi's. Rabi was old enough to be Habiba's mother although she had never borne any child of her own. When she had discovered the young

Habiba's condition soon after her marriage to their husband, and seeing that the two young girls were all by themselves and knew absolutely nothing about living alone, she came to their assistance. She saw the girl's large watery eyes as beckoning to her for help each time she passed her sitting and vomiting outside her flat. She could not turn her back on the girl and since then, she had stood by her and had seen her through a very difficult pregnancy. Inwardly, as she helped the girl, she had often prayed to Allah to answer her own prayers and bless her with the fruit of the womb. Both Habiba and Ummi were grateful for the help Rabi rendered them and since then, the co-wives had been like sisters. The boy was already fifteen months old and was named Zubairu after his father. To Habiba, no name could be more detestable to her ears but because she had no say in the choice of a name for her own child, her filial protest counted for nothing because when the time came, the little infant was named. It was a mirthless event for the young mother. On that eight day, Ummi had pronounced the name Abba which nonetheless meant father as an alternate and easier way to call the boy. Since that day, the name had stuck to him. Surprisingly, even Zubairu called him by the name, Abba.

Habiba was eighteen years; childbirth had given her young body the physique of a matured woman with heavy bosoms. She seemed more attuned to the household and Rabi, not Hauwau, had invariably become her friend and could call her to her own section of the house without notice. The other two women saw the goings-on but said nothing. Hauwau was disappointed in the fact that she and the girl Habiba could not get along. She had hoped that since Ramatu and Rabi had forged a better understanding, Habiba was going to be teamed with her. But somehow, she could not explain why she hated the sight of her, even though she was well aware that in spite of the children she had borne, she was still a more attractive woman by any standard. That the very person she thought was going to be her ally turned out to be her worst enemy without having had any quarrels since the girl came to the household gave her an astonishing feeling. All she knew was that she felt a fire burn in her stomach each time she set eyes on the girl. At some instances, the hatred she felt for the girl would keep her awake all night especially when it was Habiba's turn to sleep in their husband's room. On such occasions, Hauwau would weep in the dark until sleep stole her.

Ummi picked the child who was whimpering and calling for his mother. She wondered what Habiba had been doing that she could not rush back to her section when the rain began falling. It was still raining heavily and there was no question of going after her so she went to a table where they kept beaverages and made a cup of hot cocoa for him. First, he pushed the cup from his face, splashing the brown cocoa on the carpet that was fast losing its original lustre. Ummi kept him on the floor and swung a warning finger in his face. He sat there, tears running down his soft cheeks. He was not hungry; all he wanted was to see his mother and to be nursed on her chest.

At another section of the large compound, in a flat that seemed like Habiba's except that the paint on the walls were dirt free. Everything in the house was carefully placed and the smell of Bakhoor incense had caught the window and door blinds. It was still thundering and lightning outside. The inside of the house was dark because all the blinds were let down. There was no sign of anyone sitting on the floor or on the two cushion chairs in the parlour. In the inner room, on a large bed, under the sheets, two heads stuck out, each plaited in different styles. One was suckling the other and the groaning sounds and cries of ecstacy, mingled with the thundering outside, provided the needed balm to their desires. In this liason, there was no young and no old. The young whose chest flowed with milk from Mother Nature satisfied the thirst of the old. It had begun months after the birth of her son, Abba. Her bosom had filled and the child would not suck. The older woman had offered to help squeeze the excess milk, an exercise they had engaged in until the fourth attempt. The warm milk had spurted onto the face of the older woman and had flowed between her breasts and down through her navel to her cleavage. The warm feeling of liquid flowing into that part of her body had an aphrodisiac sensation in her brains. It was a rustic original feeling that reminded her of the original sin in the life of mankind. She looked up at the younger and their eyes interlocked for an instant. The former's eyes squinted perceptively, the younger held her head down all the time with her large watery eyes dancing in their serenity. Her hold on the soft bosom of the young mother had triggered off some primitive instincts in both women and rather than squeeze the breast, the older one caressed tenderly and licked the milk meant for the infant, first with the tip of her tongue circling round the heavy breast until she had the entire nipple in her mouth. The encouraging groans from the other had helped foster the liason until they had finally discovered the comfort of the bed.

Kraftgriots
Also in the series (FICTION) *(continued)*

Ozioma Izuora: *Scavengers' Orgy* (2011)
Ifeoma Chinwuba: *Merchants of Flesh* (2011)
Vincent Egbuson: *Zhero* (2011)
Ibrahim Buhari: *A Quiet Revolutionary* (2012)
Onyekachi Peter Onuoha: *Idara* (2012)
Akeem Adebiyi: *The Negative Courage* (2012)
Onyekachi Peter Onuoha: *Moonlight Lady* (2012)
Temitope Obasa: *Strokes of Life* (2012)
Chigbo Nnoli: *Save the Dream* (2012)
Florence Attamah-Abenemi: *A Bouquet of Regrets* (2013)
Ikechukwu Emmanuel Asika: *Tamara* (2013)
Aire Oboh: *Branded Fugitives* (2013)
Emmanuel Esemedafe: *The Schooldays of Edore* (2013)
Abubakar Gimba: *Footprints* (2013)
Emmanuel C.S. Ojukwu: *Sunset for Mr Dobromir* (2013)
Million John: *Amongst the Survivors* (2013)

Printed in the United States
By Bookmasters